# BIKER'S GIRL 3
## DESCENT TO DEBAUCHERY

by

LIA ANDERSSEN

Published by **CHIMERA**
ISBN 9781780804743

This novel is fiction - in real life practice safe sex.

# Chapter 1

The heat was oppressive. A dry, dusty heat that seemed to envelop everything about it, the sun burning down from a cloudless sky onto the parched earth of the village.

It wasn't much of a village. Fifty or sixty brown, squat huts crouched about a larger building, with chickens and cattle browsing about, trying to find something edible in the sparse grass.

Most of the villagers were seeking shade in the heat of the day, the women in brightly-coloured dresses and the men in khaki trousers and simple white shirts lounged under trees or in the entrances to their huts. The only real activity came from a group of about eight men in ragged shirts and shorts, toiling with spades and picks under the watchful eye of three gun-toting men in military uniforms.

At first there seemed nothing unusual about the caravan of horses that emerged from the shimmering heat-haze along the track that led into the village. As the people watched, they saw the ebony-skinned men sitting proud in the saddle, leading a train of heavily burdened mules that trekked through the African heat toward them. There was something unusual, though, and a murmur of surprise ran through the watching people as they saw it.

Behind one of the horses, the only one on foot, a young woman was walking. A white woman. The villagers rose to their feet as she came into view, their comments turning to shouts and whistles as she came closer. The girl was walking with her hands tied at her back with coarse rope. But that wasn't what drew the main comments.

She was totally naked.

As she came closer, the true extent of her beauty became obvious to the onlookers. She had a classically lovely face, with large, innocent eyes, sculpted cheeks and small, eminently kissable lips. She was no more than five foot three tall, with a slim, curvaceous figure. Her breasts were the size and shape of ripe oranges, the brown nipples hard and protruding, drawing the eyes as they bounced deliciously with every step she took. Her waist was thin, her hips curved. The onlookers gasped as they saw that her pubic mound was shaved clean of hair, her cunt lips visible. Their gasps turned to laughter as they realized she was tethered to the horse in front of her by a thin, coarse rope that ran from her wrists between her legs, so that it was forced up into the slit of her vagina, making her gait awkward as the chafing cord bit into her protruding clitoris. The rope was dark with her juices, and her slim legs seemed to shake as every step brought the cruel rope into contact with her most private place.

Her long, auburn hair was untidy, blowing behind her in the wind. Her soft flesh was streaked with dirt. There was a trickle of semen running down her inner thighs, revealing that she had been recently fucked. As she passed the villagers pointed to her curvaceous backside which was crisscrossed with whip marks. Even as they watched, the youngster stumbled and was rewarded with a swift cut of the whip on her bare buttocks from the following horseman, bringing a cry from her lips and laughter from the onlookers.

The crowd moved closer, hissing their disapproval of the shameless white girl as she moved past them, her face glowing, her eyes cast down. Somebody spat at her, the spittle hitting her breast and trickling down over the pale flesh. Taunts and curses were hurled, but the beautiful stranger said nothing as yet more gobs of saliva were directed at her.

In the centre of the village the leader called a halt, and the men drew up their horses. As the crowd began to close in about the nude youngster he shouted something and they backed off a little, still sneering at the girl's predicament.

Lia gazed about at the angry faces, wishing the earth would open and swallow her, rescue her from this awful degradation. To be the captive of these savage, uncaring people was bad enough. To be paraded naked before them like this, her breasts and sex on open display was just too much. The nineteen year old could not imagine anything worse. Yet she knew she could expect no mercy, and she hung her head in shame as the villagers gathered about her.

Lia was no stranger to shame, though. At an early age she had been found hitchhiking naked by the rough Bikers who were the virtual rulers of her country. Captured, enslaved, beaten and abused, she had been put through many ordeals. She had worked as an unpaid whore in a Biker club, had been the naked captive of an extreme religious group, had starred in porn films and had been abused and ridiculed wherever she went. Still, she had never imagined it would come to this.

The horseman who'd had her in tow jumped down from his steed, untying the rope from his saddle. He tugged at it, raising a laugh from the crowd as they watched the rough fibre bite into her sex, bringing a whimper from the girl.

"You like the rope on your cunt, white bitch?" he said. "You like the feel?"

He tugged on it again, pulling her to him, grasping hold of her jutting breast and squeezing it hard, pinching the nipple until she squealed with pain.

"You like that too, I think," he grinned.

He pulled the rope from between her legs and held it up to the crowd. It was dark with her juices, and Lia blushed as he ran a finger along it, then showed it to them, bringing new peals of laughter.

Whack! Once again the man with the whip wielded it, bringing it down hard on Lia's soft flesh, bringing a new cry from her.

"Fuckin' white slut," he grunted, grinning as he saw her writhe in pain.

"We're stopping here to eat," said the man with the rope. Bitches like you have to earn their food. How you gonna earn it, slut?"

Lia was hungry. She had been walking all morning, and she felt tired and weak. She wanted to eat.

"I... I could do some cleaning," she said quietly, but with little hope.

The man laughed. He reached out and took her breast in his hand, his thumb and forefinger taking hold of her nipple, which immediately swelled to hardness.

"Cleaning, eh, little white bitch? No, there is something you are much better suited to."

He turned and called to one of the policemen. Since the arrival of the caravan with its young slave the workers had ceased their toils, their eyes fixed hungrily on the beautiful girl. Now Lia felt a shiver of unease as one of the grinning guards approached, his rifle slung casually from his shoulder.

The two men conversed for a short time, with much laughter and nodding of heads. At last Lia's captor turned to her.

"You see those men?" he said, pointing to the gang of workers.

She nodded, her mouth dry.

"They are convicts. Scum. Desperate men who haven't so much as touched a woman in months, possibly years. We're giving them a little treat today."

Lia felt her stomach churn as she gazed across at the brutish looking gang.

"Please, I..."

Whack! The whip descended on her bare buttocks once more. She fell silent.

The man spun her round, and she felt the ropes about her wrists being undone. As her hands came free she rubbed the deep indentations made by the thick cord.

"Make sure you satisfy them fully, or you won't eat for the rest of the week," he muttered. He shoved her forward, stumbling towards the watching men.

Lia's legs almost gave way under her as she walked to the convicts. She knew that any sign of hesitation would be punished. She knew too what was required of her. Yet even in this desperate predicament, amongst these cruel and ugly men whose hatred for her knew no limits, she felt an odd shiver of anticipation run through her as she eyed the waiting men. Her cunt was wet with the stimulation of the rope chafing against her swollen clitoris and, as she anticipated what was about to happen, she felt a new surge of moisture seep into the heat of her vagina.

The guards stood aside and she stepped up to the first of the convicts. He was a tall man with the blackest skin she had ever seen. He wore a torn singlet and ragged shorts, and his face was wet with sweat. At first he just stared at her, licking his lips as he took in her beauty and vulnerability. Then the guard said something to him.

He reached out hesitantly and took hold of Lia's bare breast, his touch tentative at first, staring into her face as if expecting her to brush him away. Lia would have dearly loved to do just that, but she daren't, so she stood, her cheeks glowing while he caressed her soft breast.

The man turned and spoke to his companions, and they gathered about the naked girl, their eyes fixed on her bare body. Then, suddenly, they were upon her.

Hands grasped her arms, pinning them behind her whilst others groped her bare skin, feeling her breasts, making the nipples harden still further as they kneaded her pale flesh. Then rough fingers began probing, forcing her thighs apart and penetrating the warm wetness of her cunt, bringing a gasp from the

4

teenager as they violated her. Their hands seemed to be everywhere, grasping at her flesh, tweaking her nipples, probing her anus and vagina as they took advantage of her acquiescence.

Lips closed over her hardened nipples, sucking at her, making them swell into tight knobs as she fought down the sensations of arousal the assault was bringing. Lia couldn't understand the recalcitrance of her own body, her sex walls contracting about the fingers invading her, her whole body tingling with anticipation despite the disgust she felt for these unruly men.

She felt something warm and hard placed into her hand, and her fingers closed about a stiff, throbbing penis. She looked down to see that one of the men had discarded his shorts, his thick erection standing up proudly from his groin as he thrust it against her. The men laughed at the way she caressed his rampant cock, and someone shouted something she didn't understand. The scruffy convict pulled away from her caresses and laid on the dusty ground, his erection rising like a pole. Then Lia was being dragged over him by the laughing men, pulled across so that she straddled him. She looked at the villagers. Their attention was still fixed on the tableau before them, their anticipation obvious as they watched her.

The hands left her, so that she stood alone, her feet placed on either side of the man's body, her lovely breasts rising and falling as she gazed down at him. Then she began to bend her legs, crouching down over the man, dropping to her knees.

She reached out and took hold of his erection, bringing a gasp from the crowd. Lia knew they thought her a wanton slut, but she knew even better the kind of punishment she would receive from her captors if she didn't put on a good show.

Slowly, her cheeks burning with humiliation, she guided the bulbous tip of his cock to her vagina. She whimpered slightly as she lowered herself over it, trying to suppress the waves of perverse arousal that swept through her as she felt him penetrate her. Lower she went, letting his shaft penetrate deeper and deeper until she felt his coarse pubic hairs against the softness of her cunt lips.

She looked around at the convicts, who were silent now, their expressions intense as they took in her wantonness. Then she began to move, working her beautiful, naked body up and down over his penis, fucking him hard.

Lia pumped her hips against the stiff cock that filled her vagina, her movements becoming more violent, her breasts quivering up and down, the rock-hard nipples dancing as she rode out her lust on the scruffy stranger. She tried to close her mind to the hoots of derision from those watching, her own arousal building with every stroke, despite her shame and revulsion at what she was doing. Beneath her the man responded with enthusiasm, thrusting his hips up at her, watching her as she fucked him with the experienced actions of a seasoned whore.

Lia was losing control, whimpers of arousal escaping her open lips, her head thrust back, her bare breasts jutting forward as she pumped her hips up and down, the man's glistening cock spearing into her. She knew her excitement was plain to those watching, but a perverse passion had overtaken her.

The man came, ejaculating thick semen deep inside Lia's hot vagina, his big cock twitching as he emptied his balls into the naked teenager. Moments later she was coming too, whimpering with passion as she pressed down against his groin, her breasts dancing, her hair thrashing against her face as the violence of her orgasm overcame her. Then he was slowing, a grunt of satisfaction escaping his lips as he spent the last of his semen inside her.

For a moment there was silence, broken only by the panting of the naked girl as she sat, gasping, astride her violator. The onlookers were quiet too, absorbing the extraordinary sight they had just witnessed, some shaking their heads, others grinning at the licentiousness of the naked youngster.

A word was spoken, and suddenly hands were grabbing Lia again, pulling her from the man, a dribble of spunk running down her thigh as she was pulled to her feet. Moments later she found herself forced down face-first over a thick tree stump, her legs stretched wide. She gave a cry as she felt a stiff penis forcing its way into her anus. She struggled, but they were too strong for her, and she gritted her teeth as she felt her backside invaded. As the man began to bugger her another hand grabbed her hair, pulling her head round and forcing yet another erection between her lips. Lia took it inside and sucked as he thrust his hips against her face.

The ass-fucking was painful, yet even that appealed to the baser side of Lia's nature, and the taste of a thick, black cock in her mouth spurred her to new heights, her body thrashing back and forth until she was rewarded with more hot spunk in her rectum and mouth. Barely had she swallowed the last drop than she was on her back again, another erection invading her cunt while hands mauled her bare breasts and another cock was stuffed into her mouth.

The attack went on for twenty minutes as the rough convicts used her body in every way imaginable, until Lia's face, breasts and thighs were shiny with spunk. Only when the guards barked an order did the men finally withdraw, leaving her spread-eagled and panting on the dusty ground, her breasts rising and falling as she fought for control.

She rose shakily to her feet and turned to her captor, her hands at her sides, her bare breasts thrust out proudly. He grinned.

"So, you've earned your food, little white whore," he said. He turned and clapped his hands.

From one of the huts emerged two more convicts. One was carrying a bowl of steaming stew. They crossed the compound, their eyes taking in the dishevelled youngster's nudity. Lia eyed the food hungrily as they placed it down on the stump that, a few minutes earlier, she had been held over.

She made to pick up the bowl, but her captor stopped her.

"First a little garnish," he said, turning to the two new arrivals and barking an order.

The men grinned broadly, and both dropped their shorts. Their cocks stood out like thick poles from their groins. Lia gave a sigh. She had done what was asked of her, hadn't she? Couldn't they just leave her to eat?

"You can have your food when you've put some sauce on it," said the man. "Male sauce."

Lia stared at him, and down at the bowl of food. Then she understood. For a moment her stomach churned. But she was too hungry to care. Reaching out she took hold of the two convicts' cocks.

Much to the delight of those watching, the naked beauty began to masturbate the two men, her hands working them back and forth. Despite the thorough fucking she had just received, the sensation of having these warm stiff members in her fingers brought a new thrill to the wanton teenager, and she jerked the pair off with vigour, thrilling to the way their erections twitched under her ministrations.

"Remember, every drop in the bowl, or I feed it to the dogs," ordered her captor.

Lia stood, feeling small, pale and vulnerable, between the convicts, her hands rubbing their cocks vigorously, her breasts shaking as she brought the two strangers off. A gasp from the man on her right told her he was climaxing, and despite her disgust, she aimed his stiff cock at her food.

The man gave a gasp, then thick fluid began to spurt from his throbbing erection, arcing through the air and splashing into the bowl of stew. Lia pulled him forward as she wanked him, making sure that every drop of semen splashed into her meal. No sooner had his spurts stemmed to a dribble than she sensed the other man's climax. If anything he produced even more spunk than his companion, gasping with delight as he pumped his semen into the bowl of stew. Once again Lia ensured that all of his seed dripped into her meal, continuing to coax his shaft until the pulsing stopped and all the fluid had been milked.

"Clean them," came the snapped command.

Lia hesitated for a second, then dropped to her knees. She took the still erect cock of the first man and guided it to her mouth, licking the remnants of semen from his swollen glans, her saliva glistening on his rampant rod. Then she did the same to the second man, licking off every drop of spunk. Only then was she permitted to pick up the bowl of stew.

She eyed the thick, white fluid floating on top of the gravy with distaste. But she was too hungry to be fastidious, and began spooning the meal into her mouth, trying to ignore the bitter taste of spunk as she wolfed down the food, amid the laughter of those watching.

No sooner had she finished her meal than she was dragged to her feet once more and spun around. Obediently she placed her hands behind her, grimacing as her captor bound her wrists tightly. Then she spread her legs to allow the rope to be fed between them, biting into her bare cunt as the man pulled it tight.

The rope was hitched to the horse's saddle, and the men mounted up. Then Lia gave a cry as the whip lashed across her bare buttocks once more.

7

She began to walk behind the leader's horse, trying to keep up so as to avoid the pain and bitter pleasure of the rope that chafed her clitoris, semen running down her creamy thighs as she trudged along between the mocking villagers, her head down, her cheeks afire with shame.

# Chapter 2

It had only been nine months since Lia's new adventure began. Nine months in which her lovely innocent person had slipped even further into degradation in a manner she had never dreamed possible, even under control of the Bikers.

Lia had been a slave to the Bikers for what seemed forever. The Bikers were the rough, cruel men and women who maintained a pretence of law and order in the anarchic country from which she came. The Bikers were the law, despite the existence of nominal police patrols, and they ensured that things were done their way.

The unfortunate young beauty had been captured by them when she was just eighteen. She had innocently lost her clothes in a bathing accident, and found herself beside a highway naked. When the Bikers saw her and chased her down she was defenceless against them and was whipped at the roadside.

Realizing how innocent and obedient she was, the Bikers enslaved her, keeping her naked and using her as they wished. It soon became clear that the beautiful youngster, as well as being a Biker slave, was also a slave to her own desires, her body responding to any and all sexual advances. As soon as they realized her true masochistic nature they took her to market and sold her to Helda, a merciless female Biker who had her own private brothel. The calculating woman made her into an involuntary whore, teaching her how to use her body to give pleasure to the men who paid for it.

Still later Lia escaped the Bikers. Further adventures had seen her as a naked refugee, evading Helda amongst other brutal and manipulative men and women who used her even more cruelly than the Bikers, before handing her back to the female Biker who, having punished her, then turned her into a pornographic movie star.

Finally she was rescued by the one Biker who had ever shown her mercy, the blond Thorkil, who took her into his own custody.

For the next few months after falling back into his control, Lia's life was one of relative calm. The Biker proved a good master to her, and she obeyed him well, keeping his apartment clean, feeding and catering for him and, occasionally, being allowed to share his bed. Lia fell into the role of servant and sex toy with enthusiasm, always keen to keep her master happy.

All that changed, however, when one day she asked to be released from her indemnity and become a Biker proper. Thorkil had been concerned at her request. The Bikers were a tightknit group, and in order to join Lia would have to go before a tribunal, something he knew would be an ordeal. He tried to persuade her against it.

On the morning after she made the request she found herself being woken early from her bed. She slept in a small room behind Thorkil's apartment with just her basic requirements. When the bell rang twice she knew she was to attend her master naked, and she hurried to his room, shivering slightly despite the fact it was a warm day.

To her dismay she found her Biker master in bed with another woman, a Biker with an extraordinarily lovely body. She felt her cheeks redden as the woman examined her, taking in her pert breasts jutting invitingly, her nakedness making her nipples stiff with arousal and bringing a wetness to her sex. She took up a position in front of her master, her legs spread, her hands behind her head, displaying her body totally to him.

"Master?"

"This is her," said Thorkil to the woman beside him. "She wants to become a Biker."

The woman frowned. "She's a bit docile, isn't she?"

"Yes."

The female Biker stared into Lia's eyes. "You know what will happen if you fail?"

"Mistress?"

"They will find you a new master. That's the rule."

Lia felt a coldness run through her. "Master?"

"It's true, little one," he said. "I couldn't keep you."

"But if I became a Biker?"

Thorkil turned to the woman beside him, then back to Lia. "Then you could choose the Biker you slept with."

"I want to do it, Master."

"You understand the risk?"

"Yes, Master."

"Then so be it. Now go and get some clothes on."

He turned and, pulling down the sheet, exposed the Biker woman's breasts. He leaned over and began to suck at her nipple, his other hand sliding down under the sheet towards her crotch. Lia watched for a moment, pangs of envy filling her. Then she turned and left the room.

The tribunal was an ordeal. Lia was made to stand on a platform wearing only a short skirt while the men and women listened to her story. She told how she had been owned by the Bikers for some time, and how she had been an obedient servant. She expressed her love of their way of life and the pleasure it had brought her. Then Thorkil spoke, saying that despite her obedient nature he thought she would be a loyal Biker.

Then things started to go wrong. She was questioned about why she had become a fugitive from the Bikers. Why she had spent weeks hiding from them, until eventually being recaptured.

What finally destroyed her case was when Helda was brought to the stand. The cruel Biker woman showed no sympathy, castigating her for escaping, and for her attitude. She told of how submissive the girl was, describing in detail the men she had been given to. How she had allowed herself to be kept a naked prostitute, and how she had given her body to anyone she was told to give it to.

Lia's protests that she was intimidated into doing what she did fell on deaf ears, and she looked on in despair as she saw the tribunal become unsympathetic to her case.

It took only a few minutes before the committee returned and the leader pronounced the verdict. Lia was not suitable to become a Biker.

The hapless girl stood submissively on the platform while she was informed that she would no longer be in the custody of Thorkil. Instead, it was ordered that she be given to a new master, who would treat her in a manner more fitting to her lowly position. She was to move to a Biker compound hundreds of miles away, where she would become the property of a Biker called Faust. His name was familiar to her and she blanched as he climbed onto the platform beside her. He was renowned as a gruff, uncaring man whose cruelty was legend and who would prove a very different prospect from Thorkil. Indeed, his first action was to tear off her dress, then force the naked youngster to bend over while he administered twenty strokes of the cane on her bare backside, before ordering her into a small room where he fucked her.

Departing from her master had been hard. Lia had hoped to stay with Thorkil for her time with the Bikers. But she knew, too, that he would never fully return her affections, and that his kindness was just that. Any possible love she felt for him was unrequited.

From the day she arrived at Faust's place she was introduced to the realities of being a slave to a Biker. The apartment was scruffy and untidy. Faust's previous slave had been a man, who neglected his duties and ended up being sent to labour in the prisons maintained by the Bikers. Lia took nearly a week to clean the place under the watchful eye of her new master, who shouted at her and beat her for the smallest misdemeanour.

In Faust's charge life was little more than a drudge; cleaning, cooking and serving beers to the overweight Biker. She was seldom allowed out of the apartment, and even when she was it was just into the fenced compound where the Bikers made their camp. Her clothes were worn and ragged, and after her first fucking Faust took little interest in her body. To some extent this was a relief to her, although her natural libidinousness was never far below the surface and, forbidden to masturbate, she found celibacy hard to endure.

It was after she had been with Faust for about three months that everything changed for Lia. He was a relatively solitary man, preferring his own company. When he returned from patrol on his growling motorcycle he would demand a meal, then lounge about his apartment, drinking and smoking, occasionally entertaining a girl Biker while Lia was obliged to keep him supplied with alcohol and drugs.

Then one day she heard the sound of motorcycles pulling up outside. She glanced at Faust, who waved a hand, indicating that she was to go to the door. She obeyed, pushing it open nervously and gazing out, her eyes met by three strange Bikers.

The men eyed her up and down, taking in her lovely curves as she spoke timidly.

"Sirs, can I help you?"

"Where's Faust."

"Inside, Sir."

"Take us to him, girl."

"Yes Sir."

She led them in to where Faust was sitting. He rose to his feet and greeted them heartily. The three were clearly old friends of Faust, and there was much laughing and back-slapping as they made themselves comfortable.

Lia was ordered to serve them with cold beers, then to polish their already gleaming machines. Afterwards she prepared a meal, serving them and clearing up once they had eaten. It was only when she was bringing them more beers later in the afternoon that they began to take any real notice of her.

"Hey, Faust, where'd you get the bitch?" asked one of them as he took the cold bottle from Lia. He was a big, ugly man with a beer belly, who Faust referred to as Wolf. He belched appreciatively as he swigged his beer.

"She's just some slut. She was caught by a guy called Thorkil.'

"Thorkil, eh? Didn't he rescue that nympho from Helda?"

"Sure," put in another of the men, called Razor. "She made that porno movie. Never saw a bitch fuck and suck so many guys."

"Yeah, I saw that. Is this her?"

Lia heard their conversation with some alarm. She didn't care to be reminded of her lascivious past, and she felt the blood rise in her cheeks as she remembered how she had been made to behave by Helda. Picking up the empty bottles she made for the kitchen.

"Wait, bitch!"

Faust's words brought her to a stop. Nervously she turned to face the slouching Bikers.

"That true?" said Wolf. "You the fucking slut from the movie?"

Lia lowered her head. "Yes Sir," she said.

"I thought you were a fucking flasher. In the movie you go around naked all the time, flashing your tits and cunt to anyone who wants to see them."

"I... I used to be naked."

"What, all the time?"

Lia hung her head. "Yes Sir."

The man turned to his host. "Hey, how come you let her wear clothes?"

Faust shrugged. "I don't give a shit how the slut dresses," he said. "She's just a fuckin' menial."

The third Biker, Lucan, rose to his feet, a heavily built man, his arms decorated with tattoos.

"I heard she got turned on by flashing her tits and cunt," he said, his eyes traveling over Lia's shapely form. "Ain't that true, bitch?"

Lia said nothing. She didn't like the way the conversation was going at all. It had been some time since any man had taken an interest in her, and she feared the way her body would respond to the attention.

"I... I should clear up," she mumbled, turning towards the kitchen.

"Just a fucking minute."

A hand grasped her arm, pulling her back and making her drop the bottles she was holding onto the carpet. She stared apprehensively into the eyes of the Biker.

"Did you enjoy going around naked?" asked Lucan.

Lia tried to reply, but her throat was dry and nothing came out. It was true that she had been aroused by being naked amongst clothed people, but that fact caused her nothing but shame.

"'Course she fucking enjoyed it," put in another of the men. "I heard it turned her on."

"Let's take a look."

Lia glanced fearfully at the man. She wished this wasn't happening. She had grown accustomed to Faust's indifference to her, and had welcomed the fact that her underlying passions had been suppressed in his employ. Now, as she stared round at the grinning, leather-clad men, she feared it was beginning again.

"What do you say, Faust?" said the big man to his host. "Let the bitch work naked, like the slut she is."

Faust shrugged. "If you want," he said. He turned to Lia. "Strip."

Lia felt a shiver run down her spine as she heard the order. It had been months since she had escaped the humiliation of being not allowed clothes. Now the nightmare was starting all over again.

"Come on, get on with it. Get your fucking clothes off. Show us what you got."

Lia looked around at the men once more, her heart filled with dread. Then, her fingers trembling, the beautiful teenager reached for the buttons that ran down the front of her dress. It was a simple garment made of thin cotton and she wore nothing underneath. She could not remember the last time she had owned any underwear. She began unfastening the buttons one at a time, feeling the men's eyes on her, the heat rising in her cheeks.

As she worked her way down the dress fell open, revealing the creamy swell of her breasts, the nipples hardening as they pressed against the flimsy material. She reached the last button and undid it. For a moment she hesitated. Then she pulled the dress off her shoulders and let it drop to the floor. Aware that the men required her full compliance, she allowed her hands to drop to her sides and moved her legs apart. Blushing furiously, she looked shyly at the Bikers.

The men's eyes travelled down Lia's naked body, taking in the swell of her breasts. Even in these humiliating circumstances she was already feeling the first flush of arousal and her nipples were hard and protruding. Her stomach was flat, with a neat little navel. Her cunt was bare of hair, the thick lips prominent, a slight sheen of wetness coating them, her hard clitoris clearly visible.

"Very nice."

"Much better."

"Shit, look at those tits!"

"And the slut shaves her cunt."

"There, Faust, see what you've been missing?" said the Wolf. "Here, give me that dress, bitch."

Lia turned and bent down to pick up the dress, aware that the gesture gave the watching men a perfect view of her bare behind, her anus and vagina on display to all. Then the naked girl turned and moved slowly across to where the Biker was standing. Her eyes cast down, she held the dress out to him.

He took it from her and, with a grin, dropped it into a waste bin.

"Better take this out to the dumpster," he said to her. "You won't be needing it."

Lia looked at him in dismay. She had hoped the men would just want to briefly ogle her nude body, then leave her to get on with her tasks. That was her only dress, and to throw it out would be a disaster. But she knew better than to argue with her masters.

"And clear that mess," barked Faust, pointing at the beer bottles that still lay on the floor.

Once again Lia was obliged to bend over under the mocking eyes of the Bikers as she picked up the bottles. She moved across to the bin where her precious dress had been discarded.

"Wait," said Wolf. "Give me one of those."

"Sir?"

"The fucking bottle. Give it to me."

Lia sensed immediately that there was more trouble in the offing for her. Warily she approached the Biker and handed the bottle to him. Then she turned away and dropped the rest into the trash can. She made to pick it up, but froze as the Biker spoke again.

"Wait. You can do that later."

Lia straightened up. "Sir?"

"Come over here."

Warily Lia made her way to where the Biker stood, holding the beer bottle. He seemed to examine it with interest, then turned to the nervous girl.

"Ever bring yourself off with one of these?"

"Sir?"

"You know fucking well what I mean. Have you ever used a bottle as a dildo? Given yourself an orgasm with one."

"I..." Once again Lia's throat was dry.

"Well?"

13

She hung her head. "Yes."

Lia felt a wave of embarrassment as she made the confession. One of her first acts after her enslavement by the Bikers had been to stand on a stage in a crowded diner and masturbate to orgasm using a bottle. The memory of that lewd act made her shiver, as she remembered the cheers of the watching men as she frigged herself.

"Show us."

"Please I..."

"Show us."

Lia stared at the bottle he was holding out to her. She wished the floor would swallow her up. Her nudity was humiliating enough, but to use the bottle in front of these strangers...

"Do it," growled Faust.

Slowly, Lia reached out a shaking hand and took the bottle from the grinning Biker. She ran her fingers over its smooth, cold surface, a shiver of anticipation going through her naked frame. It had been a long time since she'd last masturbated and, despite the ignominy of her situation, she felt a strange sensation of arousal course through her frame, and a familiar wetness creep into her vagina.

She moved her hand down, sliding her feet wide apart so that her sex opened, bringing chuckles from the watching men. As the cool glass touched her sensitive nether lips she gave a stifled gasp, feeling those lips twitch as the perverse instincts in her came to the surface. She looked up at the three men, who were staring intently at her crotch, their faces beaming. She hesitated, reluctant to perform this libidinous act in front of the rough strangers.

"Do it, bitch."

The tone of Faust's voice told her that she faced punishment if she failed to obey. Biting her lip she took a firm grip on the bottle. Then, with a grunt, she pushed the neck up into her vagina.

For Lia it was a bittersweet sensation, having her pussy filled by the unyielding glass. On the one hand the physical sensation was delicious, her inner muscles contracting about the bottle as it invaded her so intimately. But on the other hand the shame of doing it before the watching men brought a bright flush to her face as she contemplated her disgrace.

"C'mon, fuck yourself," came the gruff order.

Lia glanced across at the men, whose eyes were fixed on her open vagina. Then, slowly, she began working the bottle back and forth inside her.

"Oh!" The involuntary cry escaped her lips as she felt a surge of arousal. She tried to fight the sensations, but her sexual desires were being kindled for the first time in months, and she knew she was losing control. A new warmth invaded her vagina as she felt the wetness flow within her. Then her hips began thrusting down against the bottle as she felt her control slipping away.

"Bitch is loving it," said Razor, his eyes fixed on the bottle as it slipped in and out of Lia's sex.

"Yeah, look at that bottle. It's covered in her cunt juice."

Lia felt her embarrassment increase as she realized that the men could see the clear evidence of her arousal. Her passion was growing with every thrust, her hips pumping back and forth as she drove the bottle into her sex, her breath coming in gasps, her breasts bouncing as she frigged herself. She could feel her orgasm building as the exhibitionist in her came to the fore and she spread her legs still wider, bending her knees to ensure the watching men got the best possible view of her naked charms.

"Stop!"

Lia barely heard the word, so intent was she on her own pleasure. Then she gave a little cry as Wolf stepped forward and snatched the bottle from her vagina.

Lia stood, her breasts rising and falling as she gasped for breath, a trickle if her sex juice running down the creamy smoothness of her inner thighs. She was totally aroused, her body screaming for relief as she stared at the object that had been filling her so deliciously only seconds earlier.

The Biker gave a chuckle and tossed the bottle into the bin.

"Looks like the bitch is still on heat," he said, and the men guffawed at the sight of the gasping girl as she slowly regained her composure.

"Dirty little slut."

"She'd let a dog fuck her."

"Maybe you should try that sometime, Faust."

Lia stood, her head bowed as the men mocked her. Then there was a slap on her bare behind.

"Go get my cigarettes."

She hurried across to the cupboard and opened it. Inside was a packet, which she took out and gave to her master. He opened it, then swore.

"This packet's empty, you stupid girl. Go get another."

"That's the only one, Sir."

"Fuck it, I could do with a cigarette," said Faust. "You guys got one?"

"We're all out," replied Lucan.

"I'll go into town and get some more," said Faust.

"No need," said Lucan. "Send her."

"What?"

"Send the bitch."

"Good idea," put in Razor.

"Okay," said Faust. He turned to Lia. "You heard him. Go get us some cigarettes. There's money and a pass on the table."

Lia glanced down at herself, then across at the trash can.

"I-I'll need my dress," she said quietly.

"Then take it out the trash can."

"Yes Sir."

"No, wait. Fuck that," said Wolf. "Go like that."

Lia stared at him in disbelief.

"But Sir, I'm naked."

"Sure you are. So what? You love showing off your tits and cunt, don't you?"

"No... I-I mean..." Lia's voice trailed away. She was totally shocked by the suggestion. Since she had been under Faust's ownership she hadn't even been obliged to show her body around the apartment. Surely this stranger couldn't be serious? She gazed imploringly at Faust.

"Sir?"

"Go on Faust, send her like that. It'll be hilarious."

Faust eyed Lia up and down, then shrugged.

"Sure. I guess it'll be a laugh. Go on, get moving."

"And if you're late we'll thrash that pretty little backside," laughed the big Biker. He took her by the arm and led her to the front door. He opened it and thrust her out, tossing the money and the pass after her. Then he slammed the door, leaving her standing alone and naked in the open compound.

# Chapter 3

Lia stood outside the apartment, looking about in bewilderment, scarcely able to believe her predicament. She was standing in the open without a stitch of clothing, her breasts, backside and pussy on open display. She had been naked in public before, but not for a long time, and she had become accustomed to the comfort of being clothed. Now, standing here, with nothing on whatsoever, she felt totally vulnerable. Worse still, the prospect of having to leave the Biker compound like this filled her with dread. But she knew she had no choice.

To her relief she was, at least for the moment, alone. She could see some men working on their bikes across the other side of the compound, but they were not looking in her direction. Still she was in an incredibly defenceless state, and she felt her stomach tighten as she realized that, sooner or later, her shameful situation would be witnessed by other people. Her heart thumping, she bent down to pick up the money and the pass. Then with extreme reluctance she set off towards the exit gate.

As she walked down the path that ran between the buildings of the compound she continued to glance right and left, aware that at any moment she might encounter somebody. She wanted badly to cover her breasts and sex with her hands, but knew that such an action would bring disapproval and possibly punishment. To her relief there was nobody around to see her. It was mid-afternoon, and she guessed most of the Bikers were taking a siesta. Still, she knew she would encounter other people when she reached the exit, and she felt a cold feeling as she approached the gate in the tall electrified fence that surrounded the compound.

As a Biker slave she would need to show the pass to get out of the compound. In her lowly position she had no right to leave the heavily protected area in which the Bikers lived. In fact, it had been some weeks since she had passed through the gates at all, and then it had been on the back of Faust's motorcycle, accompanying him to a convention in the town.

Fighting down the instinct to turn and run, Lia approached the gate. There was a single guard there. When she saw it was a girl Biker her heart sank even lower. What would she think of her, walking about with no clothes on? As she came closer the Biker looked up, and Lia saw the look of surprise on her face. Her cheeks glowing, she held out the pass.

The Biker girl took the piece of paper from her and glanced at it. Then she turned back to Lia. She ran her eyes up and down the teenager's body, taking in the swell of her breasts, the flatness of her stomach and her prominent sex lips.

"You going out like that?"

Lia lowered her eyes. "Yes. My master is sending me for some cigarettes."

"You okay with that?"

"I... yes. I must obey my master."

The Biker gave a grunt of laughter. "Shameless slut." She was an attractive young woman, about twenty-five years old, with a mane of red hair, her shapely body encased in a tight, black leather suit. Lia glanced at her enviously. She remembered how she had hoped that one day she too could have become a Biker, enjoying equality with her captors. But they preferred to use her as a domestic and as a toy. Now, standing naked before the lovely confident woman, she felt the shame of her situation even more acutely.

"Please may I go out?"

"You going into town with your tits and cunt on display?"

"Yes."

The Biker laughed again. "There's a lot of rough types out there," she said. "They're gonna think that bare pussy of yours is quite an invitation. You might get more than you bargained for."

She reached out a hand and closed it over Lia's bare breast. At once the teenager felt her nipple pucker to hardness under the touch, and she knew the Biker must feel it as well.

"Fuck me, this is turning you on, isn't it?" said the woman.

"I... I don't want it to."

"So why your nipples so fucking hard? Maybe you're gonna enjoy flashing your body after all."

"No I..."

"Forget it. Get the fuck out of here, little whore."

She pushed open the gate and gestured to Lia to go through. Lia heard the gate slam behind her, and she was alone.

The Biker compound was situated in a wooded area about two miles from the town. The first part of Lia's journey was along a track that ran down to the main highway. On either side were tall trees, and she was able to make use of them, concealing her nudity behind the trunks whenever she heard a bike approaching. She hurried down the track, constantly looking right and left, fearful that at any moment someone might see her shameful condition.

It took her about twenty minutes to reach the road, and she succeeded in hiding herself all the way, much to her relief. From there she had a further half mile in which she was still able to use the wood for cover whenever she heard a vehicle. As she came closer to the town the vehicles became more frequent, and her apprehension grew as she realized she would soon lose her cover.

Lia glanced down at her sex lips. Already she could see a sheen of moisture down there, and for the thousandth time she wondered about the perverse way her body responded to nudity in public places. Whilst her mind was filled with shame, the arousal in her body was uncontrollable. Gently she let her hand drop between her legs, teasing the prominent bud of her clitoris, sending a shiver through her naked frame. Unable to stop herself she probed her vagina, pressing her fingers into herself, a slight gasp escaping her as she did so. She knew she would soon be seen. It was a busy town, and people would be about. But why was her body responding as it was?

She leant back against a tree, her eyes half closed, legs spread as she masturbated. She might have brought herself to orgasm but for the sudden sound of a motorcycle roaring past.

She looked up as it went by, seeing it through the cover of the trees. Guiltily she withdrew her fingers from her sex. They glistened with her juices.

She shivered as she thought of where she was going. She knew that the only place to buy cigarettes in the town was in one of the scruffy saloon bars frequented by the Bikers, truckers and the lowlifes of the town. She had been taken to one of these bars once before by Faust, and forced to endure the leering eyes of the men in her thin cotton frock. But that had been nothing compared to what she faced now, naked and alone in this hostile spot.

She reached the edge of the wooded area and stopped, crouching behind a bush, peering out. The road she had to take was opposite where she was, and she could see men and women going about their business along it. She watched them, hoping for it to clear.

She remained where she was for some time, too frightened to show herself. But she knew time was ticking away, and she dare not upset her masters. Finally she took a deep breath and stepped out across the road.

At first nobody seemed to notice her, and she moved as fast as she could. But she knew she was a conspicuous sight and soon became aware of heads turning in her direction and fingers being pointed. She was on the sidewalk now, the ground warm and hard beneath her bare feet as she padded along. There was a group of men loading a truck just ahead, and already she could hear the laughter and catcalls as they watched her approach.

Lia felt her cheeks glowing, completely aware of the delightful way her breasts bounced as she walked, the hard nipples jiggling provocatively with every step. She was aware, too, of the prominence of her shaved sex.

But there was something else she was aware of. Something that increased her shame a hundredfold.

She was becoming more aroused with every step.

Why it was that baring her body brought her sexual desires to the fore was

18

something she didn't understand. She knew her nudity was disgraceful, yet to have her breasts and sex bare somehow excited her in a way she couldn't comprehend. As she came closer to the grinning men she could feel the moisture seeping from the lips of her vagina, and her nipples becoming even harder, her thoughts dominated by the image of her thrusting the bottle into her sex while the Bikers watched.

"Hey babe, you up for a fuck?"

"Sure she is. Look at that dripping cunt."

"What a dirty whore."

"Shake your ass, baby."

Lia walked past the jeering men, her eyes fixed in front of her, trying not to listen to their lewd comments as they scanned her naked body. The sensation of being stared at was almost physical to the lovely teenager, and she could barely suppress an urge to turn and run away.

She rounded a corner, and her heart sank as she saw how busy it was. People were coming and going in all directions and she was walking straight into their midst. Almost at once she was noticed, the men and women stopping and staring at the brazen youngster walking down the street, apparently oblivious to the fact that she wore no clothes. Women glared at her, or spat insults in her direction. Men laughed at her predicament or studied her bare flesh with frank desire, their eyes traveling up and down the curves of her body. The hungry stares brought new arousal as she imagined what the men would do to her if they got the chance. The sheen of wetness on her sex lips was obvious, and a shiver of embarrassment ran through her as she felt a trickle of her juices run down her thigh, the moisture gleaming in the sunlight.

Ahead of her she could see the line of seedy bars towards which she was headed, and apprehension gripped her as she knew she would have to walk inside one of them. She was amongst the shoppers now, her cheeks glowing as they stood and stared at her.

"Look at her."

"Has she no shame?"

"The little slut."

To Lia it was like a dream she occasionally had, where she found herself walking naked amongst fully-clothed people in a public place. Except this time it was real. She had been naked in public before, but never alone, and she felt totally vulnerable as she padded through the laughing, staring throng.

She recognized the bar into which Faust had taken her that time. It was a scruffy rundown place with a faded sign hanging outside and peeling paintwork. It was not the first bar in the row, and she was anxious to be off the street as soon as possible, but she resolved to stick with the devil she knew. Her eyes fixed on the sign she hurried on, only too aware of the way her breasts danced up and down with every step, her backside swaying provocatively despite her attempts to walk as demurely as possible.

She reached the door to the saloon and paused, gazing down at herself. Her nipples were standing out like knobs and, no matter how much she wished she could calm them, there was nothing she could do about it. She placed a hand on the door of the saloon and pushed it open.

Inside it was smoky and noisy. Music blared from speakers above her head, and there was a buzz of conversations. All about the room were tables at which customers, mostly men, sat drinking and talking. On the far side was the bar, surrounded by stools occupied by more drinkers. The room was crowded, and Lia felt her heart sink as she contemplated her situation.

It was only a matter of seconds before the first wolf whistle rang out. Then heads were turning and the conversations dying as the men took in the sight of the naked girl, her breasts thrust forward, the nipples standing out proudly, her sex lips shiny with moisture, her breath coming in pants as she made her way nervously through the bar.

"Hey, baby, you forgot your pants!"

"Shake those tits!"

"If you wanted a fuck you only had to ask!"

Lia tried to close her ears to the laughter and lewd comments as she approached the bar. She squeezed between two grinning men and looked across at the barmaid. The girl was chatting with some men, and seemed oblivious to the naked beauty who stood wishing she was anywhere but there, wanting more than anything to get away from the sea of eyes fixed on her bare flesh.

As she waited she glanced nervously around. There were about a dozen Bikers in the room, some she recognized. That gave her slight comfort, since she guessed she could rely on their assistance if she was seriously attacked. Most of the others were manual workers, dressed in overalls or jeans. At one table was a trio of Hispanic men, their necks and wrists decorated with gaudy gold jewellery. They were paying particular attention to her, and she experienced a new sensation of arousal as she felt their eyes upon her.

The barmaid seemed to take forever, but at last she turned. An expression of distaste crossed her features as she eyed Lia. Slowly she made her way across. Lia stood, only too aware of the way her bare breasts jutted out over the bar, the nipples still hard as nuts.

"What's your problem?" asked the woman. "Where's your clothes?" She was about twenty-five, with blonde hair and a weariness in her eyes that belied her age.

Lia's colour deepened. "I-I'm not wearing any."

"I can see that. Who the fuck do you think you are coming in here like that?"

"I-I need a pack of cigarettes please."

"I don't serve sluts."

"Please. I just need a pack. Then I'll go."

"No, stay," said the man standing beside her. "Stay a while and have some fun."

Lia turned back to the woman. "Please? Just one pack."

The woman screwed up her nose. "What brand?"

20

Lia stared at her blankly. "I don't know."

"You don't know."

"I'm sorry I..."

"You gotta choose a fucking brand you stupid bitch."

Lia felt her cheeks redden still further at the remark. She glanced about in desperation. On the wall she saw a picture of a bikini-clad girl smoking a cigarette. She read the brand name underneath.

"Camels, please," she said.

The barmaid followed her gaze. "You think you look like her?"

"What?"

"The girl in the photo. At least she covered her tits and cunt," she remarked, eyeing the girl in the picture. Then she turned away and went to a cupboard at the back of the bar.

Lia gave a start as a hand was placed on her buttock. She turned round to see a man in jeans and an undershirt, grinning through broken teeth.

"That sure is a nice ass." he said, squeezing her pert bottom.

"Please," muttered Lia. "I..."

"And it feels real smooth. You like having your ass felt?"

"No. You mustn't."

"Girl who goes around naked obviously wants it."

The man continued grinning, his hand sliding up until it cupped her breast, first kneading the soft flesh, then teasing the stiff nipple. Lia stood motionless, her hands at her sides, her fists clenched as he explored her breasts.

"Best tits I've seen in ages," he said. "It sure is good of you to share them with me."

His other hand was between her legs, rough fingers probing at her sex. Lia tried to pull away, but he placed an arm about her waist, holding her firm while he explored her vagina.

"Fuck me you're wet down there," he said. "You after a fuck or something?"

"Please," stammered Lia, squirming as his fingers delved deeper into her vagina, his thumb rubbing her erect clitoris. "Please don't."

"Shit, why would I stop? You want it bad, don't you?" he laughed.

Lia tried to fight him off, but at the same time she was finding it impossible to suppress the emotions his caresses were bringing to her. No man had touched her for months and the sensations he was arousing in her were as exciting as they were unwelcome. She felt herself weaken as her desires began to overtake her. Soon her struggles stopped, her naked body writhing as he felt her up, one hand mauling her breasts while the other frigged her.

He turned her so that she faced the other customers in the bar. Lia knew they could all see his fingers probing into her vagina, and how she was reacting, now thrusting her hips forward in a lewd dance of lust.

"Shit, what a whore."

"Bitch is gonna come."

"Give it to her good, Lou."

21

"Squeeze them tits."

Lia had lost all control, spreading her legs wide, bending her knees so that the men could get a perfect view of her vagina as her exhibitionist tendencies came to the fore. She felt an orgasm approaching and abandoned herself to the sensation, her head thrown back, her eyes staring into the faces watching her, her breath coming in soft gasps.

"Hey, buddy, the bitch belongs to the Bikers."

The words came from a heavily built man in black leathers. He had moved behind the one mauling Lia, and she gave a moan of disappointment as she felt the fingers slide out of her sex. She was so close to orgasm that her body continued its lustful dance, her hips thrusting forward as her vaginal juices flowed from her slit. She took hold of the bar, trying to steady herself as she slowly regained her composure.

"Shit, man, it was just a bit of fun."

"Yeah, well find your whores somewhere else."

"Yeah, sure. Man, I didn't know she belonged to you guys. No offence meant."

"Just go sit down."

Lia watched as her molester retreated, clearly intimidated by the burly Biker.

"Th-thank you, Sir," she stammered.

The Biker eyed her with contempt.

"Stupid bitch. That Faust should discipline you better. He send you out like that?"

"Yes Sir."

The Biker shook his head. "Boy, you are a dirty little whore."

Lia felt the blood rise to her cheeks at the words. It was true. She was dirty.

"Okay bitch, bend over that stool."

"I beg your..."

"Bend over the fucking stool!" The words were shouted this time, bringing silence to the bar.

Lia turned and looked at the barstool that had been vacated by the previous man. Shaking slightly she moved close to it, then leant over it, so that the plastic seat was pressed against her belly and her bare backside was beautifully presented to the Biker.

"Spread your legs."

Lia obeyed, her cheeks glowing as she imagined the sight she was making in the crowded bar, her wet sex and tight anus on perfect display. She glanced back, and her stomach tightened as she watched the Biker unbuckle his belt and pull it off. He doubled the leather over, then raised his arm.

Whack!

Whack!

Whack!

Whack!

The blows fell hard across Lia's bare buttocks, the leather biting into her soft flesh, bringing cries of pain and anguish from the naked teenager. The Biker showed her no mercy, using all his strength to lash the red stripes across the creamy flesh of her buttocks.

Whack!

Whack!

Whack!

Whack!

Then he was done, and Lia was draped over the stool, her body shaking with sobs at the stinging pain in her backside.

The Biker took her by the hair and pulled her to her feet.

"Now take your cigarettes and get the fuck out of here."

Lia straightened, rubbing her bum, the tears trickling down her face. She'd had much worse beatings since she became a slave to the Bikers, but almost never one so humiliating; the stinging in her bottom eclipsed by her extreme embarrassment as she glanced around at the leering customers.

She looked back, and saw that the cigarettes were on the bar. Without another word she snatched them up and hurried to the door.

So involved were the customers with the stunning beauty, her pale buttocks bearing the cruel red stripes of the Biker's belt, that nobody noticed the three Hispanic men rise from their seats and slip out of a side door.

# Chapter 4

As Lia stepped into the sunshine of the busy street she was instantly snapped back to reality, and her eyes dropped to take in her bare breasts and sex. Some of the people who had watched her go into the saloon were still there, and ironic cheers and whistles greeted the naked girl as she emerged. Other passers-by stopped in shock and amusement as they realized that the beautiful girl had no clothes on. Once again Lia felt the heat in her cheeks, and also in her sex as she contemplated the vulnerability of her situation.

All she desired now was to get back to the relative safety of the Biker camp. To be standing there, totally naked in front of all these strangers was more than she could bear.

Taking a deep breath she set off. She walked quickly, avoiding eye contact with the shoppers, but she couldn't avoid hearing their remarks.

"Bitch has been thrashed."

"Yeah, look at that ass."

"If you ask me she deserved it."

The red stripes across her backside brought new jeers and crude remarks as the people realized she had been recently beaten, bringing still more shame upon the humiliated girl. Yet she still hadn't fully recovered from the recent frigging in the bar, and still she could feel her hot sex weeping fluid as her latent exhibitionism took hold. Lia struggled to understand how she could possibly be aroused by the situation, but the recalcitrance of her body had long been a mystery to her.

She reached the end of the street and turned the corner. Once again there was no shortage of people to turn and gape at her apparent shamelessness. Still more remarks met her ears as the passers-by stared at her naked body. Lia tried to walk faster, her bare breasts bouncing as she hurried along amongst the laughing shoppers.

She was nearing the edge of town and, to her relief, the sidewalk was becoming less crowded. But still crude remarks rang in her ears as she padded along.

She crossed the highway, ignoring the horn of a passing truck, its jeering crew making lewd gestures at her as it passed. She stuck to the edge of the road, rather than try to pick her way through the trees. As she glanced up and down she saw there was little traffic. With any luck she could be on the track that led to the Bikers' compound in a few minutes.

Lia barely noticed the car as it came past, her eyes fixed ahead as she hurried along. She became aware it had stopped only when she was a few yards from it, and at once felt cold feelings of apprehension as she realized the battered vehicle was in her path.

Scarcely had she time to consider plunging into the trees when the men emerged from the car. At once she recognized them as the three Hispanics from the bar. She came to a halt, an arm instinctively covering her breasts as she stared at the trio.

"Hey, baby, wanna ride?"

Lia shook her head. "No thank you."

"Sure you do. Walk around like that you'll get sunstroke."

"I... I'm all right, thank you."

She began walking again, still trying to cover herself with her hands, but as she came close to the car the three men moved across, blocking her path.

"Please I..."

"Take a ride with us, honey."

"I-I can't."

"Sure you can."

"I prefer to walk."

"Come on baby, just get in the fuckin' car." This remark was delivered in a low, menacing tone that sent a chill through her.

"No. I..."

"Get her in the car, boys."

She felt her arms grabbed by strong hands. One of the men said something in Spanish. Then she was being dragged towards the open car door.

"Please! Please don't!"

"Shut the fuck up."

Lia struggled as best she could, but she was no match for the three strong men, and in seconds she found herself being bundled into the back seat of the car. The doors were slammed, and with a squeal of tires the vehicle was speeding down the highway.

The frightened girl was jammed between two of the men, and she glanced anxiously at them. All three of her kidnappers were in their mid-thirties, with swarthy complexions, their narrow eyes gleaming as they studied their helpless captive. Each wore bright gold jewellery about his neck and wrists, which clinked noisily with every movement.

"Wh-what do you want of me?" asked Lia, her voice shaking.

The man on her right grinned, showing discoloured teeth.

"You know what we want. You bin showing it to us ever since you walked bare-assed into that bar."

"Please. Don't hurt me."

He grinned a crooked grin. "We won't hurt you if you do as we say."

Lia looked at him, then his two companions. She knew she was helpless. She knew they would get their way with her whether she complied or not. These were rough labourers, and they obviously saw her as fair game.

Lia bit her lip, then turned to the man next to her.

"Will you let me go if I do what you want?"

The man laughed and said something in his native tongue, bringing laughter from his companions. Lia knew they were amused by her obvious compliance, the heat rising in her cheeks as they took in her naked charms.

"You gonna be obedient?"

Lia lowered her eyes. "If you don't hurt me."

"Shit, we don't wanna hurt you. We wanna give you what you want."

"You'll let me go when you're done?"

"Sure. Just do as we say."

Lia closed her eyes. "I'll do what you want."

"Right, little whore," he hissed. "Open your legs."

"Please, I..."

"You said you'd do what we want. You backing out on that?"

"No. I just..."

"Then do as you're fuckin' told," grunted the man on her left "Spread your legs and show us what we're getting."

Lia gritted her teeth. She knew she was giving in too easily, but she had committed now. She was in the control of the men and she must obey. Slowly, reluctantly, she moved her knees apart, her cheeks glowing as she revealed her pussy to the watching men. She knew they could see how moist she was, a trickle of fluid running down the pale flesh of her inner thighs. She lowered her eyes in shame at her brazenness.

"Nice cunt for a gringo."

"Look how wet she is."

"This babe needs it."

The car made an abrupt turn to the right, into the forest along a rough track. She wondered where she was being taken. At least they were not going too far from the Biker compound, she thought.

"You like to fuck?"

The question came from the man on her right. He was leaning over her, his eyes traveling over her bare breasts and down to the cleft between her legs.

Lia said nothing.

"Answer me. You like to fuck?"

Lia's cheeks were crimson. "I..."

"I think you like," said the grinning man. "Girl who walk about like that showing off her tits and cunt to everyone is asking to be fucked. You asking to be fucked?"

Again Lia didn't reply, but she knew there was a ring of truth in what he said. To brazenly walk the streets naked, her arousal obvious to all, was just an invitation to trouble, and trouble was what she now had.

The man ran his hand up the soft flesh of her thigh, making her jump at the sudden sensation. Her instinct was to push his hand away, to tell him not to touch her. But her training from the Bikers came to the fore and instead she made no move to stop him, her hands resting at her sides, her legs still apart.

His fingers found her sex.

"No hair down here," he said. "You a very dirty girl."

He probed her nether lips, bringing a gasp from the beauty as his rough hands sought out her clitoris, which had swollen into a solid bud.

"This hard and wet," he remarked, rubbing it gently.

Lia gritted her teeth, trying to ignore the delicious sensation of being touched so intimately. "Please don't," she whimpered, unable to stop herself from spreading her legs still further as he slid a finger into her vagina.

For her it was an extraordinary situation. She was both frightened and disgusted by the coarse men who treated her with such contempt, acting as if it was their right to maul her naked body. But her physical response belied her shame. What made things worse was that it had been many months since she'd had even the smallest of sexual encounters. Now her enforced nudity was arousing feelings she'd not experienced in a long time, and the coarse fingers exploring her vagina were almost too much for her. Trying to stifle a moan she writhed slightly as she felt her juices flow anew.

The man fingering her said something to his companions, bringing fresh laughter from them. Both the other men were watching her reactions with obvious amusement. The driver had adjusted his mirror so that he could see exactly what was going on, and Lia knew they could tell she was clearly aroused by the man's caresses. He pressed his fingers deep into her sex, while his other hand caressed her bare breasts, bringing gasps from the lovely girl as her naked body squirmed under his touch.

Suddenly the car swung to the left, onto a narrow, bumpy track. It continued for about a quarter mile, lurching through the potholes, then came to a stop. Lia had scarcely been paying attention to where they were, so absorbed was she in the crude fingering her pussy was getting. She glanced out the window and saw they had stopped outside a rundown building. It was a bungalow, once a nice house, she thought. Now though it showed all the signs of neglect, the porch sagging, the windows broken.

The man withdrew his fingers, bringing a soft moan from the aroused girl. He held his fingers up in front of her face. Lia blushed as she saw how wet they were. He showed them to his companions, who commented crudely. Though she couldn't understand what they were saying, she knew they were mocking her.

The three men opened the car doors and climbed from the vehicle, then stood shoulder to shoulder staring at their lovely captive.

"You coming out, babe?" asked the man who had been touching her.

"Sure she's coming out. She don't wanna fuck in the car, do you honey?"

Lia hesitated, reluctant to leave the car, wishing desperately for some salvation from what she knew was to follow. She glanced down at her nakedness, blushing at her erect nipples and the sheen of moisture on her thighs.

"C'mon babe. We got what you want out here."

Lia hesitated a moment longer. Then, reluctantly, she too pulled herself out.

She stepped onto the lush grass. It felt soft and cool beneath her bare feet. The sun shone down on her naked flesh, bathing her in a glow that she might, in other circumstances, have enjoyed. But at the moment she was far from enjoyment. She was alone and naked in a remote place, standing before three men whose jeans were bulging at the crotch, and she knew what was required of her.

Whoring was not unknown to her. Not more than a year before she had been innocent and chaste. Then she had fallen into the hands of the Bikers, who used her body in every way imaginable. For many weeks she had literally worked as a whore, in the club owned by the cruel Biker girl, Helga, who delighted in keeping Lia naked and selling her to her customers. But she escaped from the wicked dominatrix, and had vainly hoped those days were behind her. Now she knew they weren't.

One of the men said something to her, then gestured at the front of his jeans. Lia pretended she didn't understand what he wanted, staring at him with innocent eyes. But his words needed no translation.

"My cock needs sucking, bitch."

"I-I..."

"You know the agreement. You obey us and you won't get hurt."

"Yeah, go ahead and suck him. You gonna love the taste of a Latino cock."

Lia held back for a moment longer, then slowly moved close to him, until her • jutting nipples almost brushed against his shirt.

"Taste it, girl. You know you want to."

Lia dropped to her knees and reached for his zipper, her hand shaking slightly as she pulled it down.

She delved inside his fly, her fingers feeling the hardness of his shaft straining against thin briefs. Gently she pulled them down, allowing his cock to spring from his pants. It was rock hard, thick and circumcised, the end solid and shiny. She stared at it for a moment, her fingers closing about his shaft, a thrill running through her as she examined the twitching erection.

"Look. It's turning the bitch on."

The man's comment was accurate. She felt a surge of lust at the sight and scent of male arousal, grasping his rod and moving her hands up and down, causing a bead of lubrication to seep from the tip. Hardly thinking what she was doing, the lovely teenager leant forward and took him into her mouth, sucking hard as she ran her lips down his stiff erection.

She heard a murmur from the men, and glanced up to see them grinning down at her. She knew what a slut she must seem, but there was no turning back now. They had seen her lust, and would use her as they wished.

It was then that she finally abandoned herself to her desires. She reached out a hand for the crotch of the second man, even while her head was pumping back and forth on the first. She heard a snort of laughter as she ran her fingers over his bulging crotch, and glanced up to see the third man watching, a broad grin on his face. Oblivious to his mocking tones she sought the zipper on his jeans, pulling it slowly down. Then her hand was delving inside, seeking out his thick penis. In no time she had a second cock in her hand and was stroking the foreskin back and forth, to the obvious delight of the man.

She felt her free hand taken and her fingers closed about a third pulsing shaft. She knelt there on the grass, her hands and mouth filled with cocks. She sucked hungrily at the one between her lips, loving the way the ones in her hands twitched as she played with them. Her libidinous nature was taking over, her lovely body responding to the men. Between her legs she could feel her sex lips convulsing, forcing more fluid out onto her thighs as she pleasured the trio, her stiff nipples rubbing against coarse denim and sending new tremors of excitement through her.

A hand took hold of her hair, pulling her head back so the erection of the man in front of her slipped from her mouth. She gazed up at him, her hands still caressing his friends' stiff cocks.

"You ready for fucking now?" said the man.

Lia nodded dumbly, bringing a fresh smile to his lips.

"Little slut."

He shoved her back so the penises in her hands slipped from her grasp. She sprawled onto the grass, laying on her back and gazing up at the threesome. The depravity of what she was doing struck her, and she felt the urge to jump to her feet and make a run for it. But she dismissed the plan almost as it came to her. She was committed now. Committed to fucking three strangers in the deserted wood, where nobody would hear her cries.

Slowly she spread her legs apart, revealing the wetness of her cleft to the trio, reaching a hand down and rubbing her clitoris with a finger. She bent her knees and raised her bare ass from the grass, offering her naked body to the three men. She peered between the valley of her breasts at them, moaning slightly as

28

she continued to masturbate.

They stood for an instant, their eyes traveling over her luscious curves, clearly delighted by her submissiveness and wantonness. Then the one whose cock she had been sucking stepped forward and knelt down between her open thighs.

Lia took her fingers from her vagina and reached for his erection, now anxious to feel a real live cock inside her. The fact that it was a stranger violating her didn't seem to matter anymore. For the first time in months she was able to surrender herself to a man, and that was what her body needed. Slowly she drew him closer, pressing his shining glans against the slippery entrance to her vagina and raising her buttocks higher to assist his entry.

She gave a moan of desire as she felt his thick shaft slide into her, the muscular walls of her fuck-hole pressing against the invader, as if trying to suck him in further.

"You like Latino cock?' he said.

"Yes," she gasped.

"You want me to fuck you?"

"Yes. Fuck me hard. Please."

He began a slow, rhythmic pumping of his hips, bringing a fresh cry from the teenager's lips as she felt his cock slide back and forth inside her vagina. She could see the other men watching, and she knew her response was shameful, but she was no longer in control of her desires, writhing and gasping beneath him as he began to thrust into her.

As he found his rhythm he began to fuck her with gusto, ramming his hips against her, using her body for his pleasure, clearly enjoying the uninhibited reaction of the teenager as she gasped and moaned her desire beneath him. Lia knew they must think her a total slut, but she didn't care now. All she cared about was the exquisite pleasure of being filled by the dark-skinned man, and being fucked so dispassionately.

He was moving faster, his grin turning to an expression of total desire as he enjoyed her naked body. She could see the same intense expressions on the faces of his companions too, and thrust her pelvis up with renewed force against him, her luscious breasts shaking with the violence of his onslaught.

Lia was gasping with desire, her entire body throbbing with lustful excitement as his thick cock pounded into her. Somehow the fact that she was being fucked publicly, naked in the open, brought new waves of perverse excitement to her, her hips thrusting upward as he plunged his erection deep into her.

She sensed his passion increasing, his thrusts becoming harder, his muscles tightening. Then he was coming, his cock shooting gobs of hot semen deep inside her vagina. Lia could scarcely remember the last time she had enjoyed the sensation of a man shooting his spunk into her. It was the most extraordinary sensation for the lustful youngster and seconds later she was coming too, her body convulsing as she screamed with pleasure, her head rolling from side to side, her backside thrusting with renewed energy against him.

So lost was she in her own climax, she scarcely noticed as he slipped his shining cock from inside her and rolled aside. Then she was brought back to reality with a gasp as she felt a fresh erection plunging into her open pussy. She opened her eyes to take in the leering face of the second man as he violated her without thought for her. He began to fuck her and to her surprise she cried out again as another shattering orgasm swept through her ravished body.

The next half hour was a blur to the lovely girl as the men used her beautiful body, pumping sperm into her vagina and mouth, laughing at the way she moaned and screamed, bringing her to orgasm after orgasm with their stiff cocks. Lia responded with an enthusiasm that shocked even her, abandoning herself totally to their desires, swallowing their spunk with relish even as more was pumped into her sex.

When at last they'd had enough, they forced her to her knees and made her use her tongue to clean their cocks of spunk and vaginal fluid. Then they simply hitched up their pants and wandered into the cabin, leaving her spread-eagled on the grass, spunk oozing from her vagina, her exhausted body covered in sperm, grime and grass stains.

For some time Lia was unable to move, her ravaged body supine, her breasts rising and falling as she regained her breath. It was fully ten minutes before she raised her head and looked about.

She rose slowly to her feet, stretching her aching limbs, trying not to contemplate the shamefulness of her actions. She looked across at the house. It was clear that the trio was done with her, and that she was free to go. A sudden wave of shame shook her, making her shiver as she contemplated how she had acted, giving her naked body to the uncaring men. She had to get away from there. Away from their scornful gazes and mocking laughter.

She glanced about. She knew which way they had come in the car, and she guessed her best chance of finding the Biker compound was to retrace her steps. She began walking down the track, then stopped. She hurried back to the car. There on the seat was the pack of cigarettes. She retrieved it, then made her way back through the wood.

# Chapter 5

The walk back to the camp was a lonely one, a fact for which Lia was grateful. The fewer people who saw her the better, in her mind. As she walked she pondered her behaviour of the last hour. The men had taken her and used her, but in her heart she knew she'd been consensual to the sex, and her body responded to it with enthusiasm. She had come many times, and made no attempt to fight off the men. They called her a slut, and she wondered if the word was accurate.

She had been walking for nearly fifteen minutes when the throaty roar of a bike met her ears. She paused for a second, her heart thumping, as she was reminded that soon she would have to present herself to the Bikers again. The sound of the motorcycle came from somewhere ahead of her, and told her she didn't have far to go. Despite her dread of what Faust and his companions would say when they saw her, she knew she had been gone far too long and quickened her pace.

One thing she was certain about; she could expect a punishment from the Bikers, especially when they saw she'd been fucked. Even masturbation was forbidden to her, and she felt her cheeks glow anew as she contemplated facing them in her current state, but she had no choice.

She had been walking in shade. Ahead she could see the brightness of sunshine. Then she pushed aside a low-hanging branch and found herself on a wide path. The tracks of motorcycle wheels in the dirt told her she was close to the compound.

She heard another bike approaching from behind with some speed. For a second she contemplated diving back into the bushes and hiding her nakedness, but decided against. It was only a matter of time before she would have to face her masters. There seemed little point in delaying it.

She stood at the side of the track, her legs apart, hands at her sides, listening as the bike came closer. For a second she was reminded of the day when her nightmare at the hands of the Bikers had begun. Then too she had been naked, standing on the highway, masturbating as a truck approached, her shameless behaviour guaranteeing the vehicle would stop. She felt a fresh spark of arousal as she remembered her brazenness, standing naked on a public highway, her legs apart, her knees bent, thrusting three fingers into her wet sex in clear view of the approaching truck. It was how the Bikers found her and, realizing her libidinous nature, had enslaved her.

Her reverie was shattered as a pair of gleaming motorcycles rounded the bend. For a second she almost lost her nerve, but she stayed where she was, watching as the two men caught sight of her and immediately slowed, bringing their machines to a halt in front of her.

"What the fuck are you doing out here?"

The man who spoke was about forty, with a thick beard and pronounced paunch.

"I... I was sent to get some cigarettes. My master is Faust."

The Biker eyed her up and down. Lia felt shame rising as he took in her nakedness, her filthy state and, worst of all, the streak of semen that ran from her shaved labia down her legs.

"You been fucking?"

She nodded. "Y-yes, Sir."

"With a Biker?"

"No Sir."

"How many men?"

She bit her lip. "Three, Sir."

The other Biker shook his head. "Dirty little bitch. Let's take her in."

"Damned right we'll take her in. Right, slut, turn around. Put your hands behind you."

Lia's stomach churned as she saw him unhitch a pair of handcuffs from his belt.

"Turn around I said!"

Obediently she turned and put her hands behind her. She felt the cold steel of the cuffs close about her wrists. Her hands trapped behind her, she turned to face the Bikers again.

He reached out a hand and grasped her breast, squeezing it roughly, pinching the erect nipple, clearly enjoying the expression of pain that crossed her face as he did so.

"That's not the only pain you're gonna feel, you little whore," he hissed. "Now get on behind me, and make it quick."

Lia went to the rear of the bike. Mounting it wasn't easy without the use of her hands, but she managed it, avoiding the leering eyes of the other Biker as he watched her swing her leg over, affording him an unrestricted view of her bare pussy and the spunk that still leaked from it. Then the bike's engine roared, and they sped away.

It took no more than a couple of minutes to reach the gates of the compound. There Lia was forced to face the Biker woman who had let her out. She felt ashamed as the woman surveyed her ravaged body.

"I told you not to go out like that," said the woman. "I guess you wanted to, though."

Lia said nothing and was relieved when she opened the gate and they roared inside. Once again, as they rode along, Lia was subjected to the stares of the Bikers. There were many more around now, and they pointed and laughed as she was driven, naked and cuffed, towards Faust's apartment.

They pulled up outside and cut the engines.

"Get the fuck off, and make sure the seat's clean."

Lia dismounted. She glanced down, and the blood rose in her cheeks as she saw the wet imprint of her pussy there, a mixture of spunk and sex juice forming a glistening design. The biker was looking at it too.

"Clean it!"

Slowly she leant forward, her luscious breasts dangling as she bent over the seat. She put out her tongue and began lapping at the bitter fluid.

"That's it. Make sure you don't leave any."

Lia cleaned every drop from the seat as the Bikers watched. By the time she had finished the door had opened and Faust and his three companions were standing there, gazing at the dishevelled youngster.

"What the hell happened to you?" asked Faust.

"Bitch has been fucking," said the Biker who had delivered her. "Looks like more than one guy."

"She sure had a good time," said the other Biker. "Look at her."

"You should keep an eye on the slut," put in the first Biker. "Okay, bitch, give me back my cuffs."

She obeyed, standing quietly as her hands were freed. Then a shove in the back sent her stumbling towards her master.

"Hope you punish her good," the Biker laughed.

With that he kicked his machine into life, and he and his companion rode off, leaving her head bowed, her hands at her sides.

"Where are my cigarettes?"

Lia had almost forgotten the original purpose of her mission, yet she was clutching the packet in her hand. She held them out to the Biker, who snatched them from her.

"What the hell happened?" said Faust again.

"I... there were some men."

"What men?"

"They were in a car. They pulled me inside."

"And you let them?"

"I was afraid they'd hurt me."

"So they took you in their car. Where?"

"Just into the woods. Then they made me get out."

"And then?"

Lia hung her head. "Then they..."

"They fucked you?"

"Y-yes."

"You fucked them willingly?"

"There were three of them. I couldn't fight them off."

"So you didn't try?"

"I... I wanted to, but..."

"Did you come?"

"Please, I..."

"Did you come?"

She hung her head. "Yes."

"How many times?"

"I-I don't know."

Whack!

Lucan had pulled his belt off, and delivered the naked girl a stinging blow across her thigh.

"Dirty slut!" he growled. "Who were they? Describe them."

Lia knew that if she described her attackers they would be easy to find. There were few Hispanics in the area. She knew, too, that the Bikers would show the men no mercy. She looked at Faust.

"They were Hamites."

"Hamites? You dirty little slut!"

Lia knew the Bikers would be shocked. The Hamites were a group the Bikers particularly detested. They were originally from Africa, proud, with a great tradition of seafaring. Their ships carried goods from Africa to the seaports, where there were always Hamite villages. There the ships were serviced and cargoes unloaded. As well as the Hamites, the seaports tended to be inhabited by seamen from other parts of the world; a rough, lawless crowd. The Bikers always stayed away from these ports, content to control the trucks that carried the goods from the docks inland.

Their hatred of the Hamites was little more than simple racism. They distrusted them and considered them inferior. For their part, the proud Hamites loathed the Bikers. The dominance of the Bikers inland meant that few of the Africans ever ventured far from the coast. It was not unusual for the police to arrest them on suspicion of crimes they had no connection with, and once found guilty many were handed over to the Bikers to work as slave labour. Indeed, Lia was the sole white slave in the compound, the rest being Hamite labourers.

To admit she'd had sexual intercourse with Hamites was something she knew would disgust the Bikers, but she didn't want to be responsible for the way in which the Latinos would be treated for using a Biker girl as they had. As she faced Faust and his companions she could see the repugnance in their faces.

"You let those bastards have you?" growled Faust incredulously.

"You let them stick their black cocks in you?"

"Have you no shame?"

Lia lowered her eyes. She was beginning to regret what she'd said. The three Bikers were outraged. "I didn't have a choice," she mumbled.

"But you let Hamites have you."

"And they made you come."

"I-I couldn't stop them."

"But you fucking came!"

Wolf suddenly grinned "Well, since she obviously likes that Hamite shit, maybe she should be treated like one," he said.

"What do you mean?" asked Faust.

"She's got her own quarters here?"

"Sure. It's a room out back. She's locked in there at night."

"Why not put her with her own kind?"

"Her own kind?"

"The Hamites."

Faust shook his head. "You're kidding."

"Take a look at her. It's where she belongs."

Faust eyed the dirty, dishevelled girl, taking in her untidy hair, the dirt and grass marks on her flesh and the streak of semen running down her thighs. A faint grin crossed his face.

"Maybe you're right."

"Sure I'm right. Go give the warder a call."

"Yeah. Call the warder."

Lia listened to the exchange in silence, her heart pounding. The area in which the Hamite slaves were kept was a concrete block, with tiny cells separated by iron bars. It was worse than any prison, with squalid conditions and a cruel regime. Surely they wouldn't subject her to such conditions?

"Get inside and clean yourself up," Faust ordered her. "Then come see me."

Whack! His hand came down hard on Lia's bare behind, sending her scurrying into the house.

She made her way back to her sparse quarters, a room with a mattress on the floor, with a small bathroom attached. She climbed into the shower and turned on the tap, giving a sigh as the water cascaded down onto her. The shower was a release. A chance to wash the three men's fluids from her body, and to lather off the grime of the fucking. She soaped her breasts and sex, grateful to be away from the lustful eyes of the men, if only temporarily. The water was no more than lukewarm but she revelled in its flow, feeling relaxed for the first time since Faust's companions had disturbed her life.

All too soon, though, she was done, her body clean once again. She wiped herself dry with a thin towel, then paused for a moment before a mirror, taking in the full swell of her breasts and the curves of her body. She eyed her crotch, wishing it wasn't denuded of hair. Having a shaved pussy made her appear a total slut, as well as emphasizing her pussy lips and the way her clitoris protruded when she was aroused.

She glanced about the bathroom for something to wear, but there was nothing. Time was passing, and she knew she must return to her masters. She hoped they had at least come inside the apartment, but Faust's front room was empty and she realized with a sigh that she would have to go out and stand naked in the open once again.

As she stepped from the doorway something caught her eye. Something that brought a fresh pang of anxiety. There was another motorcycle at the front of the house, and a man was talking to the Bikers. His name was Rocca, and he was warden of the slave quarters.

Lia felt a shiver run down her as she felt his gaze fall on her nude body. He was a tall thin man, with long dishevelled hair and two days' growth of beard. He grinned as he caught sight of her.

"This the bitch?"

"Sure is," replied Faust.

"Where's her clothes?"

"Yeah, where's your clothes, slut? You after getting fucked again?"

The other Bikers laughed, bringing a new glow to Lia's cheeks.

"She comin' like that?" asked Rocca.

"Sure. Little slut loves to walk about bare-assed. Gives her a thrill."

The warden laughed. "It'll give those Hamite bastards a thrill as well."

"She's already done that today, dirty little bitch," said Wolf.

Faust turned to her. "Come here, you."

Lia obeyed, her eyes cast down as she stood in front of Rocca. She moved her legs apart, and let her arms hang at her sides in a gesture of submissiveness.

"I got a nice little cell for you, babe," said Rocca, his eyes betraying his amusement. "It's right among those Hamite scum. You'll love it."

"Bitch still needs thrashing, though," said Wolf.

"Yeah," said Faust. Lia shivered as she saw him reach for his belt.

"Nah, not like that," said Wolf, putting a hand on his arm. "Rocca here's got that in hand, haven't you?"

"You want me to use the X?"

"Sure. With that special attachment you were talking about."

"Special attachment?" said Faust.

"Sure. She's gonna love it. You comin' down to watch?"

"Yeah."

Rocca pulled a walkie-talkie from his belt and spoke a few words into it. Lia listened with some alarm. She wasn't sure what they were discussing, but she knew that whatever it was it meant something unpleasant for her.

Rocca put down the radio and turned to her.

"Give me your wrists."

The warden pulled a pair of handcuffs from his saddlebag. They were attached to his bike by a chain about seven feet long. Lia looked at them in alarm.

Whack! "Give him your fucking wrists." The slap by Faust on Lia's bare ass made her shriek. Obediently she stretched out her arms, shivering slightly as the cold steel snapped about her wrists. Rocca started his bike.

"Hope you're a good runner," he sniggered, then slipped the clutch and the bike roared forward, with the naked girl frantically running behind, the Bikers' laughter ringing in her ears.

# Chapter 6

As Lia stumbled along behind the motorcycle she barely had time to see where she was being taken, intent as she was on staying on her feet. Word had spread at the camp about the beautiful young slave and her behaviour that afternoon, and on either side of the track were laughing Bikers, who cheered as the naked youngster loped past them, taking long strides with her slender legs, her breasts bouncing with every step.

Rocca was clearly enjoying himself, and Lia was dismayed to see he was not heading directly for the slave block. Instead he took her around the camp, in the sight of more jeering Bikers. She wondered how much longer she could keep going, the sweat running off her bare flesh. She knew that if she fell the Biker would show no mercy, and the thought of being dragged along the ground naked was not one she cared to face.

A building came into sight. Lia had never thought she would be relieved to see that ugly block. It was squat and grey, the walls topped with vicious looking razor wire, the windows barred. Now, though, it was a welcome sight to the exhausted girl.

The Biker gave one final spurt of speed, almost pulling Lia of her feet. Then he pulled up his machine at the entrance to the building and Lia was at last able to come to a halt, gasping for breath as she recovered from her ordeal.

For long moments she took no interest in her surroundings at all, leaning against the back of the bike, her breath coming in whooping gasps. Her energy had been drained by the ordeal, and it took a long time before she began to recover. Only once her breathing became more shallow did she look about, and what she saw made her heart sink.

The prison-like structure was where most of the slaves on the compound were housed. Along the thick wall were small windows lined with iron bars. From behind the bars Lia could see dark faces peering out. What an extraordinary sight she must be making to them; a naked girl, her wrists shackled in front of her, her body on view for all to see. She knew that letting the Hamite slaves see her like this was part of Rocco's plan to humiliate her. No Biker woman would show herself to the Hamites, whom they hated.

Lia turned her eyes from the imprisoned men, and gave a start as her attention was caught by something else, and a cold shudder ran through her.

In front of the gated entrance to the building was the 'X' to which Rocca had referred. It was a wooden frame that formed an X-shape, with leather straps attached at the extremities. She had seen the structure before, and knew it was a whipping post, though she had never seen it used. She saw a muscular Biker, stripped to the waist, standing beside it. In his hands was a thin cane, and he flexed the weapon menacingly as he stared at the lovely captive.

Rocca went across and spoke to the man. Lia could tell they were talking about her from the way they kept glancing across at her, and she felt her heart sink as she saw the smile spread across the other man's face. Then Rocca approached her.

"Okay, you know what that is?" he said, pointing to the frame.

"Yes Sir."

"And you know what it's for?"

"Yes, Sir."

"And you think you deserve a thrashing?"

Lia didn't reply, lowering her head.

"Twelve strokes, I think," he said, his lips curled in a cruel smile.

Lia shivered, but again said nothing. Since becoming a slave of the Bikers she knew that compliance was her only option. Any dissent would only make things worse for her. She stood quietly while Rocca undid her cuffs, then allowed herself to be led naked to the frame.

As she walked she glanced about. News of her public punishment had clearly spread and Bikers were approaching from all sides. There were men and women, most clad in the leathers that were the uniform of the Bikers, and Lia felt her cheeks burning as they pointed at her naked body, laughing and joking at her predicament.

Lia walked up to the frame and stood facing it, waiting for the order to press herself against it. The crowd gathered about her.

Rocca turned to them. "This slave is known to have spent the afternoon being fucked by a bunch of Hamites," he said.

"Shit!"

"She fucked more than one of them?"

"Dirty slut."

Lia noted the expressions of disgust on their faces.

"So we're giving the slut twelve strokes to teach her a lesson," continued Rocca.

A murmur of assent came up from those watching.

"That's what she needs."

"Beat some sense into her."

"Only twelve? She deserves more."

Lia stood, naked and alone, sensing the hostility of her captors. But Rocca hadn't finished.

"It seems the bastards brought her to multiple orgasms," he said. "How many times did you come, girl?"

Lia hung her head. "I-I don't know."

"Five times? Ten?"

"I'm not sure."

Another murmur came up from those watching.

"Since our miscreant likes being fucked so much, we're trying out something new on her," said Rocca.

He turned to the shirtless man, who bent down and reached into what looked like a sports bag at his feet. He pulled something out and held it aloft for the onlookers to see. As Lia stared at it she felt a chill in the pit of her stomach.

It was a phallus. About eight inches long and more than an inch and a half thick, it was made of wood, and had been carefully carved into the shape of an erect penis, two thick veins running up the shaft, the tip swollen and smooth. As he showed it to the watching Bikers Lia heard their laughter, and shivered as she contemplated the purpose of the ugly device.

Rocca turned to her. "You know what that is?"

"It - it's a penis, Sir."

"Yeah. Just what you like."

"Couldn't you get her a black one?" shouted one of the Bikers, bringing fresh laughter from the crowd.

"You know what it's for?"

"I can guess, Sir."

Having made sure that everyone had a good look at the phallus, the shirtless man turned to the wooden frame. Just below the centre, where the two beams crossed, was a hole. The false cock had a bolt protruding from the base, and he inserted it in the hole. A few turns and it was fixed in position, rising at an oblique angle.

Rocca turned to a pair of Hamite slaves, standing beside the frame.

"Right, you two, mount the bitch."

Lia wasn't given any more time to consider her fate. She felt her arms grasped. She looked to either side. The two large men, dressed in the ragged clothes of Hamite slaves, grabbed hold of her. At Rocca's order they lifted her off her feet. They were powerful men and Lia's struggles were to no avail as they raised her over the projecting phallus.

"Get it up her."

Lia's legs were dragged apart, exposing her bare lips still further. Then, amid the cheers of the crowd, she was slowly lowered onto the thick pole.

Fingers penetrated her sex, forcing her portal open, then pressing it down against the bulbous tip of the cock. Lia gave a gasp, and then a moan as she felt the inert object penetrate her in the most intimate manner possible. Deeper and deeper it went, forcing her vagina walls apart, bringing unexpected and unwanted pulses of arousal to the lascivious youngster as she felt herself filled. Her face was suffused with blushes as she was so publicly impaled, and the laughter of those watching rang in her ears as she felt her sex lips pressing against the wood of the frame, and she knew the false cock was all the way inside her.

"Right. Secure her."

The men took hold of her ankles, dragging them downwards, pressing the cock still deeper inside her. Then leather straps were attached to them and tightened so that they bit into her flesh. Once secure, her arms were pulled above her head and similar straps wrapped about her wrists.

When they finished Lia was helpless, her naked body stretched crudely apart, her breasts pressed hard against the coarse wood, chafing her nipples and causing them to pucker. But it was the wooden cock inside her vagina that was holding her attention, her shame at her nudity increased tenfold by the crude device pressed up inside her.

Rocca checked her bonds, letting his hands run down her flanks, briefly caressing her pert buttocks, so beautifully displayed to those watching.

"Twelve strokes will decorate this pretty ass nicely," he murmured to her.

Lia said nothing. She was no stranger to beatings, nor to humiliation, although she had hoped that the days of disgrace and degradation were behind her. But tied securely, her naked body spread, her cunt filled with a thick dildo, she braced herself for what was to come.

Her eye caught one of the Hamite slaves who had seen to her bondage. He was a tall man, well over six foot six, slim and muscular. Despite the raggedness of his clothing there was an air of dignity about him that made the girl uncomfortable. He stared at her through narrowed eyes, his expression one of contempt for the shameless white girl. Lia dropped her gaze, suddenly a little afraid of the arrogant man.

The shirtless man reached into his bag again. This time he withdrew a long thin cane. He flexed it, bending it almost double, then swishing it through the air. The sound brought a pang of anxiety to Lia as she knew her punishment was about to begin.

"Give it to her."

"Thrash that pretty ass."

"Show her what we think of women who give themselves to Hamites."

Her punisher moved round behind the helpless girl. She lowered her eyes in embarrassment as she contemplated the sight she made, the rounded cheeks of her bottom presenting him with a perfect target, the thick pole of the phallus embedded in her vagina. The man paused, she felt the cool bamboo tapping against her buttocks, and she closed her eyes.

Swish! Whack!

The cane came down across her bare bum with terrifying force, making a sound that echoed from the buildings as it struck her. For a second there was a white stripe across her bare flesh. Then at once it began to darken to an angry red.

Swish! Whack!

Down came the cane again, the second stripe forming a flat cross with the first. Lia clenched her fists as the pain hit her, her eyes tight shut, her body taut.

Swish! Whack!

The third stroke was aimed downward over the top of her buttocks, biting into the tender flesh and leaving another livid mark on her otherwise unblemished skin.

Swish! Whack!

Swish! Whack!

Swish! Whack!

The pain was almost unbearable and, despite the futility of it, Lia found herself tugging at her bonds in a hopeless attempt to avoid the cruel cane.

But there was another sensation too.

Every time the cane struck Lia's hips were thrust forward by the force of the blow. And every time that happened the phallus was forced deeper into her vagina, causing her sensitive clitoris to chafe against its surface and bringing an unwanted pang of arousal to the lascivious youngster. Lia could never fathom the recalcitrance of her body. She wanted to be modest and demure, but she had been cursed with a sex drive that was seemingly insatiable. This, combined with her masochism and exhibitionism meant she was unable to control herself when manipulated in this way.

Swish! Whack!

Swish! Whack!

Swish! Whack!

"Shit, look at her pumping."

"She's fucking that damned cock."

"Bitch is on heat."

The comments and laughter from those watching told her they'd noticed the effect the beating was having on her. Even through the terrible pain of the caning she felt her hips begin to gyrate, forcing her down on the wooden cock with increasing urgency. Her erect nipples were chafing deliciously against the coarse wood of the frame as she rubbed back and forth, groaning with arousal.

Swish! Whack!

Swish! Whack!

Lia was barely able to keep count through the fog of pain and sexual stimulation, but she was vaguely aware that the beating was almost over. Still she thrust her hips, the pain in her backside somehow urging her on in her lascivious onslaught on the rampant wooden phallus.

Swish! Whack!

For the twelfth time the cruel cane cut into her naked flesh, bringing a scream from the helpless girl. Then a new sound emerged from her lips, a mewing, moaning as she thrust her hips down on the hard rod that filled her so deliciously.

"Go it babe!"

"Shit, she's gonna come."

Lia clenched her fists as her body arched back and a fresh moan escaped her lips. An extraordinary orgasm overcame her, her cries ringing out as she bucked and writhed, the juices flowing from her sex and running down the wooden shaft.

Lia's body shook helplessly as her orgasm pounded through her, her ears filled with the jeers and laughter of the watching Bikers as they realized she was coming. Slowly, though, her gyrations subsided as she finally began to regain control of herself until, at last, she was slumped against the wooden frame, her breath coming in short gasps, her body bathed in sweat, a trickle of love juice running down her naked thigh.

# Chapter 7

Lia hurried down the dusty path that ran from Faust's apartment to the slave compound, her head down, ignoring the grins and whistles of the Bikers as she passed. She knew the hour was growing late, and she was anxious not to miss the curfew at the prison, aware that to do so would mean further punishment.

As she walked she tried hard to retain her modesty. It wasn't easy. The grey and stained prison shirt she wore had tears in the thin material that revealed tantalizing glimpses of flesh. The back of it barely covered her backside and the buttoned front threatened to part, revealing the lips of her shaved pussy. The sides were slit up almost to her waist, and it barely contained her full breasts, the top few buttons missing, revealing her cleavage and the upper slopes of her luscious orbs, the nipples pressing against the fabric.

She supposed she should be grateful for any kind of garment. In fact, after her encounter with the Hispanic men and the awful punishment she had received, she almost expected to be kept naked as she had been by the Bikers on previous occasions. Still, the meagre shirt, worn with no underwear, left her exposed and embarrassed as she hurried on, futilely tugging at it to keep herself covered.

It had been nearly a week since she had been forced to give up her modest little room in Faust's apartment for a dingy cell in the prison. It had proved to be a fresh ordeal for her. She was the only female slave in the compound, and it was certainly not designed for mixed sexes, built for males only. The cells were set in a circle, with the guards' post above looking down into them. Each cell was separated from the next simply by iron bars, so there was no privacy from the eyes of the guards or her fellow prisoners.

The Hamite slaves were kept three to a cell. Only Lia had a cell to herself, for which she was grateful as she felt the lustful eyes of the sex-deprived men on her at all times. Because only bars separated her from the other prisoners she was obliged to stay away from the sides of her small cell, where arms stretched out to grope her at every opportunity. At night she could feel their eyes on her as she tried to sleep, curled up on her blankets. When the guard post was unmanned, as it was for short periods in the night, the men would whisper obscenities to her and, on a number of occasions, she was splashed with semen as someone in the next cell jerked off over her scantily-clad form.

Thankfully, though, the other prisoners were not permitted to come close to her. She was allowed to eat her meals at Faust's apartment and to return to her cell at the curfew time. Still she felt vulnerable amongst the leering men, and she was only too aware of their sexual desires.

She particularly feared Mbosa. He was the big, proud man who had helped secure her to the frame for her caning. He had an air of aloofness about him that clearly awed even the other slaves, and it was rumoured he was some kind of chief in his own country. He made no secret of his hatred of the Bikers, obeying their demands with obvious disdain and often giving his own orders to the other slaves. He treated Lia with utter contempt, and she tried to avoid his gaze at all times, the memory of the public orgasm in his presence making her cringe with shame every time she saw him.

Lia felt her feet dragging as she approached the forbidding prison building. She glanced at the clock above the entrance. She only had two minutes to beat the curfew, yet she was more than usually reluctant to enter. Before letting her out that morning Rocca had come to her cell. He made her stand, legs apart and hands behind her head in a stance of submission with which the young slave was only too familiar. The pose pulled up the hem of her shirt so that her pussy was exposed to him. She had been only too aware of the eyes of the other prisoners fixed upon her as she stood while he inspected her. It had been a great relief to her when he dismissed her, allowing her to head off to Faust's place.

She entered the prison and walked up to the desk where a fat, bearded Biker was sitting, his feet resting on the table. She recognized him as Karl, one of the regular jailers. He was in conversation with two others, a man and a woman. Lia knew the woman as Katia. She had seen her around the compound. Indeed Katia had once visited Faust's apartment, and Lia remembered the intense way the woman watched her as she carried out her chores. Now she felt a new wave of embarrassment as the female Biker eyed her.

Karl glanced at his watch as she came in.

42

"Cutting it a bit fine tonight," he grunted.

"I - I was finishing my work."

"You should do it quicker."

"Yes Sir."

Lia began to make her way past him.

"Wait!"

The order came from Katia, the female Biker. Lia came to a halt, looking questioningly at her.

"How do we know she's not smuggling a weapon in?" said the woman.

Karl grinned. "She ain't that bright."

"Still, I think you should search her."

"Yeah," said the other Biker. "I think so too."

Karl's grin widened. "Okay, come over here."

Lia made her way back to where the three Bikers sat, feeling very apprehensive.

"Okay, take off the shirt."

The teenager paused, gazing at the two strangers. She had been strip-searched before on entering the prison, but then she had been taken into a small cell. Here, in the entrance, with these strangers watching, she hesitated

"Get the fucking shirt off!"

There was no mistaking the authority in his voice. She knew she would have to obey. Slowly she began undoing the buttons, working her way down to the bottom, all the time feeling the amused eyes of the Bikers on her.

"Take it off."

For a second she hugged the garment to her body. Then, reluctantly, she let it slide down and drop to the floor. The blood rose in her cheeks as the three Bikers took in her breasts and shaved pussy lips.

"Give the shirt to me."

Lia bent down to pick up the garment, then handed it to the slouching Biker, who grinned broadly.

"Like showing off what you got, don't you, slut?"

Lia said nothing, her cheeks glowing.

"Arms out, legs apart."

She did as she was ordered, her stomach churning.

"Turn around. All the way."

Lia could see that her little display was already causing some interest outside the entrance hall. A number of her fellow slaves were gazing at her naked body from doorways inside the building, and one or two passing Bikers were also watching. She tried not to think of the eyes upon her as she slowly revolved, giving them all a view of her curvaceous backside before turning to face them again.

The Biker laughed. "Okay," he said, holding out the shirt. "We've seen enough."

"No wait a second, Karl," said Katia.

Lia looked up in consternation. Katia had placed a hand on Karl's arm. She rose to her feet.

"You sure she's not hiding something somewhere else?"

Lia eyed the woman fearfully. She was about twenty-five and a full six inches taller than Lia, her height enhanced by the high-heeled boots she wore. She was clad in a one-piece leather outfit that hugged the curves of her body, accentuating her full breasts and slim waist. Her hair was black, framing a face that would have been beautiful were it not for the danger in her green eyes and the cruel set of her mouth.

She moved close to Lia, and the teenager gave a gasp as she placed the flat of her hand on her bare belly.

"You hidin' anything in that pretty pussy of yours?" she demanded.

"N-no, Ma'am."

"You won't mind if I check then? Get into the office."

"The office, Ma'am?"

"Yeah. Go in there and sit on the desk. Then spread your legs. Move!"

Lia gave a start at the shouted order. She glanced at the office door.

"Move I said, you stupid slut!"

Lia hurried across the hall and into the small room. It was drab and lit by a single bulb. In one wall was an opening, covered by a tatty old curtain. The desk had a bare surface of unvarnished wood.

"On the desk!"

Tentatively Lia turned and perched her buttocks on the edge of the desk, shivering slightly at the sensation of the wood on her bare flesh.

"Spread!" ordered Katia.

Lia did as she was told, positioned so she was facing the door, where half-a-dozen or so Bikers gathered to watch, and she heard their sniggers as she moved her thighs wide apart. The rough treatment of the guard and his companions had already aroused her perverse masochism and, as she felt the petals of her sex open, she knew the wetness inside would be visible to all.

Katia moved close and again put her hand on Lia's bare flesh, this time on the smoothness of her inner thigh, bringing a gasp from the girl at the intimacy of the touch. She shut her eyes, trying to blot out the pulses of arousal that were beginning to grip her.

"Look at me."

Reluctantly Lia did as she was told, staring into Katia's green eyes.

"You like being touched?"

"I..."

"Sure you do."

The woman began to slide her hand up Lia's thigh.

"Oh!' Lia let out a slight sigh as she felt Katia's fingers touch her sex lips. The woman smiled at her obvious arousal.

"That's where you really like to be touched, ain't it?"

"Please, I... ah!"

44

Another cry escaped Lia's lips as the female Biker slipped a finger into her vagina. Lia knew the woman could feel the heat and wetness inside her. She wanted to turn away, hide her face, but she knew she was obliged to keep eye contact with her tormentor.

"You really want it, don't you?"

Lia said nothing, aware only of the finger that gently probed her sex and the many eyes watching the violation.

"You like to fuck with girls?"

"With girls?"

"You know. People with tits and cunts."

"I... I don't know."

Lia knew her true sexuality lay with men, and that the sensation of a cock in her cunt or mouth would never fail to set her on fire. But the caresses of this beautiful dominant woman were having an extraordinary effect on her, and she felt her hips gyrate as a second finger probed into her weeping vagina

"I reckon you'd like to fuck with a woman. I reckon you'd like to fuck with anyone."

Katia leant forward and pressed her fingers deeper into her sex, bringing a fresh cry from the transfixed girl.

"You like this too."

The woman began to caress Lia's breasts, her fingers teasing the hard nipples.

"Kiss me, slut."

Katia closed her mouth over Lia's and her tongue snaked into the teenager's mouth.

All at once Lia was overcome with desire, her backside rocking against the table as she urged the woman's fingers deeper. Her whole being was absorbed with the scent of the statuesque Biker, whose long tresses brushed her cheeks as they kissed, her hands continuing to stimulate her spread body.

Then abruptly the caresses stopped and the woman stepped back. laughing. Lia gave a gasp of disappointment, her legs wide, her breasts rising and falling as she fought to regain control.

"We gotta get it on, pretty little slut," murmured Katia. "Let you taste some real hot pussy." She went to the office door. "Show's over guys," she said, giving the onlookers a little wave.

"Aw, come on Katia."

"Go find your own action." She closed the door on their disappointed faces. Then turned back to Lia. "Now for some real fun," she said.

Her hand went to the zip at the neck of her suit. It was already low, so the swell of her breasts was visible, the deep cleavage revealing creamy flesh. As Lia watched in fascination she pulled the zip lower, all the way down to her crotch.

Katia let the suit open, and Lia licked her lips as she saw what was revealed. Beneath it the woman was naked, her breasts sprung out, the erect nipples set on large areolae. Letting her gaze drop, Lia took in the woman's dark thatch of pubic hair, and the cleft slit.

"Like what you see, slut?" She moved close again. "Wanna taste some tit?"

She grabbed Lia's hair and forced her face between her breasts. Instinctively the teenager searched for a nipple, and sucked it between her lips. She sucked urgently, her tongue flicking back and forth, the bud puckering even harder under her ministrations. She found herself reaching for the other breast, squeezing the pliant flesh and teasing the nipple between finger and thumb. She knew all too well the thrill of having her breasts played with, and found herself deeply excited as she indulged herself in perfumed flesh.

Katia's breath was shortening, and a low moan escaped her lips as she pressed her breasts against the girl's flushed face.

Lia switched her mouth to the other breast, continuing to suck with enthusiasm, her hands squeezing and caressing the too, her arousal increasing as she felt the woman's growing too.

Suddenly Katia pushed her away, then peeled the leather suit off down to her boots.

"On your knees," she ordered. "Time for you to taste some pussy."

Obediently Lia slid off the desk and knelt, her eyes fixed on the woman's crotch. Katia spread her legs as far as the restriction of her lowered suit would allow, bent her knees slightly, then took hold of Lia's hair once more and pulled her close. Lia was immersed in the scent of female arousal. She gazed for a moment, adoring the thickness of her sex lips and the faint sheen of wetness. Then she began to lick.

"Harder... suck my clit."

The Biker pressed Lia's face into her crotch, opening her legs wider. Lia began to probe her tongue into the woman's vagina, the taste of her juices bringing a thrill to her as she worked. She sought out the hard bud of Katia's clitoris and, closing her lips about it, sucked greedily. She licked again, pressing her tongue deep, drawing gasps of pleasure from the woman.

She reached round and cupped Katia's buttocks, running her fingers between them as she feasted on her sex. The woman was grinding now, small cries coming from her lips as she became more and more turned on by the actions of the lovely slave.

She came with a moan, new wetness leaking from her cunt onto Lia's upturned face as the girl continued to lick, her tongue darting in and out of the woman's vagina.

At last Katia's moans began to subside as she sank back, her bottom resting against the desk. Lia licked the last traces of her cunt juices from her thighs, then sat back on her haunches, gazing up at the Biker. She was extraordinarily aroused and desperately wanted to masturbate, her own juices leaking onto her thighs.

There was a clatter from behind the curtain-covered opening.

"What the fuck?" Katia pulled up her leathers, struggling back into them. "Karl, get in here!" she shouted as she pulled up the zipper.

46

The door opened and Karl burst in. He paused for a second, taking in the kneeling girl, her face wet with love juice, then Katia staring at the curtain.

"What's up?" he said, looking bewildered.

"Someone's in there," said Katia.

"What?"

"In there. I heard someone."

Karl moved around the desk, listening. "Shit, you're right." He wrenched the curtain aside and grabbed an arm, pulling a man into the room. "What the fuck you think you're doing?"

It was one of the black slaves, and Lia realized with embarrassment that he'd been peeping on her and Katia. Now though, he looked wide-eyed and scared as he glanced at the two Bikers.

Karl threw him back against the wall.

"Sir, I didn't mean to..." he babbled.

"Dirty swine was in there all along," spat Katia.

Karl took the man by the scruff of the neck. "Don't you realize this woman's your superior?"

"Yes, Sir."

Karl indicated Lia. "Dirty little slut like this one's even too good for your sort to be spying on."

"You gotta make him pay, Karl," Katia goaded.

"Listen, I didn't see nothing," stammered the frightened man.

"Shut your fucking mouth. It's the solitary cell for you tonight, then tomorrow you'll get what's coming to you."

"Should cut off the bastard's balls," Katia urged.

"Yeah. Might just do that."

Still protesting his innocence the man was led away. Lia watched in silent dismay, knowing how cruel the Bikers could be. She wished she could help him, but there was nothing she could do.

Katia threw the shirt across to her.

"Cover yourself up, slut," she ordered. "Even your tits and cunt are not for the likes of him."

# Chapter 8

"You! In here!"

The words caught Lia by surprise. She'd felt she was alone as she made her way down to the bathroom. Normally as the only female in the cell block she was allowed fifteen minutes to herself in the evening, when no other prisoners were around.

She turned, and her heart leapt as she saw she was facing Mbosa, the senior Hamite. He was standing at the door to the laundry room, and she realized he had been working in there. Normally he would be obliged to keep the door closed at this time. What could he want of her?

"Inside!" he growled. "Now!"

"But I..."

The teenager's arm was grabbed by the hulking man and she was dragged bodily into the laundry room.

"You mustn't," she protested as he closed the door. "If they catch you they'll punish you."

"Like Walagu?"

"What?"

"Walagu. You tempted him earlier with your whore's body."

"Oh, please, that wasn't my fault."

He looked down at her with disdain. "You shameless slut."

"It wasn't me. It was Katia. I just..."

"You just performed a lesbian act with her. It wasn't Walagu's fault. He was just tidying the cupboard, as he'd been told to."

"But what could I do?"

"Because of you Walagu will probably lose his balls."

"They wouldn't, would they?"

"You don't understand how they treat my people. He's accused of attempted rape of a Biker woman. For that they'll castrate him."

"Rape? But he didn't come near either of us."

"You think they care? He's a black man and he saw you licking that woman's cunt. That's enough for them."

"I... I'm sorry, but what can I do?"

"Oh, you can do something. In fact, if you don't Walagu won't be the only one to suffer, I can promise you that."

Lia looked at the man. He was glaring down at her and she felt a shiver of fear. "Please, don't hurt me," she said quietly.

"You won't get hurt if you do as you're told. We have to get Walagu out of here."

"Help him escape? But how?"

"With a little help from a slave slut. Now, if you know what's good for you you'll listen carefully."

# Chapter 9

Lia lay in her cell, her heart pounding, her eyes open. She couldn't sleep. Not facing the prospect of what was expected of her by the Hamites.

Above her cell she could see the light from the room where the guard kept vigil. Faintly she could hear the sound of a TV. She wondered again when the man would make his rounds.

It was a common routine, played out every night that around midnight, the guard would circulate the cells, checking the locks and shining his torch in on the unfortunate slaves. Lia had no idea what hour it was, but she knew the time must be close, and felt a shiver run through her as she contemplated what she must do.

She heard a chair scrape back. Moments later a head appeared briefly looking down at the cells. Then it was gone, and her stomach muscles tightened as she realized the time had come.

Lia rose silently to her feet. She reached for the buttons of her shirt, slipping them undone. Then, with another shiver, she peeled off the shirt and dropped it on the floor.

She moved closer to the barred door of her cell, then lowered herself to a sitting position. The cold stone floor felt strange against her naked flesh, but she lay back, then spread her legs, bending her knees, feeling the cool air on her sex as the lips opened. She took a deep breath, then slid a hand down between her legs, penetrating her vagina and teasing her clitoris, feeling it harden under her touch. She began to masturbate.

Under the Bikers' strict code she was forbidden to bring herself to orgasm, and she knew she could be punished for this lewd act. She knew too, though, that from the next cell Mbosa would be watching her. And she feared him as much as she feared the Bikers.

She suppressed a groan as her vagina responded to the urgent rubbing of her fingers. Despite the fact that she was performing under pressure and despite her fear of the consequences, her body was responding, and she felt the familiar waves of arousal flowing through her. She knew that at any moment the guard would be down in the cell block and would see what she was doing, and somehow her perverse nature found it strangely exciting and, almost without thinking what she was doing, her other hand slid up to her breasts and began massaging the soft flesh, feeling her nipple harden at once.

She heard a key turn in the lock, and a creak as the door opened. The entrance to the block was almost opposite her cell and she knew she was about to be discovered. Even if the pale form of her wasn't clear, the gasps and moans escaping her lips would draw him to her, and the thought of being caught in this lewd situation brought a new spasm of excitement to her.

"What the fuck...?"

He was at the bars to her cell, and with a shock she recognized the voice of Karl. The glare of a powerful torch flicked on, its beam aimed at her open sex. Her fingers began to work harder, making an audible squelching sound as her juices flowed anew.

"Shit. You frigging yourself, bitch?"

Lia raised her head, looking straight into the beam of the torch, her face a picture of sexual arousal as she continued to slide her fingers in and out of her sex.

"Fucking stop. You ain't allowed."

"I... I can't," she gasped. "Please..."

"I'm coming in there."

She heard the sound of a key in the lock. Then the powerful Biker was beside her, staring down at her spread, naked body.

"Stand up."

"I... I..."

"Stand up I said!"

Karl grabbed her arm, snatching her fingers from her hot sex and pulling her to her feet. "What the fuck you playing at?"

"I'm sorry. I... I need it."

"You need it, eh? I'll show you what you need."

Still holding her arm in his left hand, the bulky man reached down and undid the zip of his jeans. Moments later Lia found herself staring at an uncircumcised erection, twitching as he took in her naked charms.

"Suck it, you little whore."

He thrust her down so she was kneeling before him. Lia gazed at his erection for a moment, then wrapping her fingers around it, she took it into her mouth.

It was thick and rigid, and tasted of male arousal, and she ran her tongue back and forth over the tip, snaking it around his foreskin and licking his swollen glans.

"Fuck, that's good," murmured the Biker. "That's what a bitch like you is for. Suck it harder, that's it."

Lia moved her head back and forth, sucking the stiff penis that filled her mouth, relishing the taste of the man's arousal, her dislike of him forgotten as she consumed him. But she knew she needed to go further, that before long he would fill her mouth with spunk, and she needed something else if Mbosa's plan was to be accomplished.

She took her hand from his dangling balls and ran it down between her legs, caressing the hard bud of her clitoris. The move was not missed by him.

"You want something meatier in your cunt?"

"Mmmm." Lia nodded her head, only too aware of the outrageousness of her reaction. The Biker laughed, then took hold of her hair and dragged her mouth off his cock.

"You hungry for a fuck, babe?"

"Yes. Yes please."

Lia made herself sound as eager as she could, though if truth were told she really was aroused and the thought of a sturdy cock inside her, even the coarse Biker's cock, brought a new thrill of excitement to her.

"Get down on your back and spread your legs."

"No. Do it to me over there."

"What do you mean?"

Lia took hold of his hand and pulled him over to the bars that separated her cell from Mbosa's.

"Fuck me here," she said, leaning back against the metal and spreading her legs, thrusting her shaved sex forward.

"Shit, you're a dirty little whore," he grinned. "I'm gonna enjoy thrashing your ass for this behaviour. Come here."

He took hold of the naked teenager and lifted her up. Lia felt his cock pressing against the entrance to her sex. She reached down and guided it into her wet vagina.

"Ah!" She couldn't suppress a cry of arousal as she felt herself filled by him. He pressed her down, sinking it deeper and deeper into her until she could feel his coarse pubic hair against her labia. Then pressing her hard against the bars he began to fuck her in earnest, thrusting his hips and drawing fresh gasps from her.

Mbosa's plan was almost forgotten as Lia lost herself in the excitement of rough sex. Every thrust banged her against the iron bars with force, yet all she could think about was the delicious sensation of being fucked hard, her legs wrapped around his waist, her breasts pressed against his rough jacket, the nipples erect.

"Fuck me you've got a tight cunt," grunted the Biker. "Get ready to have it filled with spunk."

The words spurred Lia on, her breath coming in short grunts as she felt her orgasm approaching. She thrust her hips forward, relishing the thought of his sperm pumping into her.

Thump!

The noise of the blow brought a fresh gasp from her. For a second she felt the Biker's body go stiff. Then he was falling, pulling her down with him, his cock still deep inside her, turning as he fell so that his body was across hers, trapping her beneath his bulk. Lia gazed up to see Mbosa staring down at her, the wooden club he had used to fell the Biker in his hand. Then he was reaching through the bars and unhitching the ring of keys which dangled from the Biker's belt.

Lia's mind was a whirl. Just seconds ago she had been on the verge of a shattering orgasm and, even as the Biker's cock softened inside her, she could feel her wetness seeping out, her nipples hard as nuts, her gasping breath still short as she tried to control her desires.

She began to struggle to get out from under the heavy bulk. Slumped as he was, unconscious across her, his body was a dead weight, and despite wrestling with him she was unable to get up. Mbosa was gone.

Moments later she heard a voice beside her and looked up to see two faces staring down at her. She recognized them as the two who shared Mbosa's cell. For a few seconds they simply stood, grinning down at the trapped beauty, then they were grabbing hold of the unconscious Biker's arms and legs and lifting him off her.

Lia felt herself pulled to her feet. One of the men took hold of her arms, forcing them behind her while his companion ran his eyes over her naked form. Lia felt the blood rush to her cheeks as she felt the men's eyes upon her. She knew they had watched her being fucked by Karl, and that they'd been denied contact with a woman for many months. She tried to shrink back as the one in front of her reached out and began to caress her breasts, making the nipples harden anew under his rough hands.

51

"Please..." she said, "I must dress myself."

The man's grin widened, but still he said nothing, his hands travelling over her soft globes while his companion continued to hold her.

Suddenly Mbosa was back with them, and alongside him Walagu. He barked something to the two men, who looked at him for a moment. Then Lia felt her arms freed as the pair stepped away. She glanced anxiously at Mbosa. He gave her a condescending glance, then knelt down by the unconscious Biker. There was a pistol at his waist, and he pulled it out and slipped it into his pocket. Then he snatched a pair of handcuffs from his belt, which he threw to Walagu, giving a sharp order to him.

Lia felt her arms grabbed again and pulled behind her. There was a snap as the handcuffs were fastened about her wrists.

"Wha...?" she gasped.

"You will be hostage in case of trouble."

"But I've got no clothes on."

"Just keep quiet! Now move! We're getting out of this place!"

# Chapter 10

Lia's heart was beating hard as she followed Mbosa up the narrow staircase that led out of the cell block. Her fear was infused with embarrassment as she thought of the view she was giving the following three men, her naked behind right in front of their hungry eyes. She knew they'd been denied any form of sex for months, possibly years, and the sight of her must be extremely tempting. Her only comfort was that Mbosa was concentrating on escape, and was clearly superior to the other three.

They reached the lobby to the cell block, and Mbosa made them hang back while he reconnoitred the way ahead. Moments later he was waving them forward and Lia found herself stepping out into the open, glancing nervously about, almost as concerned about her nakedness as by the fear of being caught escaping.

There were no Bikers in sight. Mbosa led them across to a building where it was dark, then turned to them.

"Now it get dangerous," he said.

"Wh-what are we going to do?" asked Lia.

Mbosa glared at her. "You keep quiet and do as I say." He waved a hand in the direction of the main gate. "We go that way," he said. "Shoot our way out."

"No!" squealed Lia.

"You do as you're told, slut," hissed the man. "We use you as hostage. They not shoot us."

Lia looked at him, then down at herself. She knew the Bikers wouldn't consider her valuable enough to trade for these men. Besides, they'd assume she'd sided with the Hamites, and with their racial prejudice so strong the Bikers would have a very low opinion of any girl who did that.

There was another reason for her reluctance, though. She knew there was a better way for them to get away. But did she dare show them? Putting herself into the hands of such desperate men was not a good idea, she knew. She guessed too that once out of danger they would want to fuck her, and there'd be little she could do to stop them.

But the alternative was no better, so nervously she turned to Mbosa.

"I know another way," she said.

"I told you to keep quiet."

"But there's another way out of here."

"How?"

"There's a place in the north of the camp. Some renegades got in there once."

"What do you mean?"

"They dug down and got under the fence. I was there when they got caught. It was never properly repaired."

The man moved close to the girl, taking hold of her arm, his grip wrenching a gasp of pain from her.

"I know white people hate black men like me. This is a trick. You trying something on."

"No. I... I want to help you."

His expression of contempt increased. "You want to help black men?"

Lia's face reddened, aware that the others were watching her closely.

"Y-yes," she said. "I want to help you."

Walagu reached out and ran his hand over her naked breast. Lia suppressed the natural reaction to push him away, bringing a smile to his lips.

"I think she want black cock," he said.

Mbosa glared down at her for a moment longer. Then released her.

"You show us."

Lia led them across to a dark pathway that ran between the buildings. She knew her way around well, having been in the encampment for months, and she was aware of where most of the Bikers would be at this time. The four men followed, Mbosa immediately behind her.

They walked for a few minutes. Every now and again they would cross a bike track and Mbosa would make them pause while he checked the way was clear. Once they came across a small group of Bikers sitting outside a building drinking beer, and were forced to make a detour. For Lia it was an agonizing journey, only too aware of the men's eyes on her naked backside and of her extreme vulnerability, her hands cuffed behind her, her body openly available.

At last they reached the edge of the encampment, where the fence rose up above them. Mbosa took her arm and swung her round to face him.

"Now, where this place?"

Lia surveyed the fence. It all looked different in the darkness and she struggled to recall the day when the breach had been made.

"I think it's further along," she said.

"You think?" Mbosa's expression was suspicious. "I thought you knew."

53

"It is further. This way."

The man hesitated for a moment, then followed as she made her way along the fence.

Then, with a sigh of relief, Lia saw the place she was looking for. "Here," she said.

Mbosa crouched down at the point she had indicated. "There is nothing here."

"Just dig down a couple of inches."

He scraped away at the dirt, then gave a grunt. He slid his fingers under the fence and pulled. The mesh lifted, leaving a narrow gap beneath. Lia breathed more easily. She had been pretty certain the breach had never been properly repaired, but was relieved all the same.

Mbosa looked across at his companions and said something to them. One by one the three lay down and rolled under the narrow gap.

"Now you."

Lia hesitated. This was her one chance to escape, she knew. If she turned and ran now there was only Mbosa who could catch her, and she knew that if she made a noise it was unlikely he would chase her. At the same time she feared what the Bikers would do to her if she left the compound without permission.

But she knew she was already too deep in trouble to remain. Her seduction of Karl, and the fact that she had led the men to the weak point in the fence meant she had burnt her boats. She had little choice but to do as Mbosa told her. She lowered herself to the rough earth, then she was rolling under and being pulled to her feet by the men.

They held the wire, allowing Mbosa to follow, then they were moving off into the cover of the woods that surrounded the encampment.

They walked on for about five minutes, then came to a stop.

"Stand over there, against the tree."

Lia stood, her legs apart, her breasts thrust forward, only too aware of the effect her naked body was having on the men.

Mbosa turned to his companions. A discussion followed that Lia was unable to understand. She guessed they were talking about the next stage in their escape, and from the way they kept turning to look at her she was obviously the subject of some debate. She shivered slightly as she listened to their voices, wondering what fate would befall her in their hands.

At last they seemed to reach agreement, and Mbosa turned to her. "We need to get away fast," he said. "You will just hold us up. We are going to leave you here to find your own way."

"Leave me?"

"Consider yourself lucky. I want to get rid of you for good, but these three are more merciful. You can stay here and fend for yourself."

"But the Bikers..."

"That's your problem."

Lia stared at him. Much as she feared the Hamite and his colleagues, and much as she realized how they would use her given the chance, she knew she would have a better chance of escape if she remained with them. Left here, naked and alone, it was only a matter of time before she would be recaptured.

"Please," she begged, "take me with you."

A slight smile crossed Mbosa's face as he glanced down at her breasts.

"You want black men?"

"I... I want to escape."

"I think you just want black cocks inside you."

"No..."

"You think these three won't fuck you?"

Lia's face reddened. "I don't know."

"Of course you know."

"Please."

"You will hold us up, slut."

Lia looked into his eyes, searching for sympathy, but found none. Then an idea struck her. "I know where there's a car!" she enthused.

Mbosa stared at her. "What?"

"I know where there's a car. Here, in the woods."

He moved close to her. "Tell me."

"There's some men. Three of them. They live in a place here in the woods. They have a car."

"How do you know?"

"I met them once."

"You met them?"

Lia felt the heat rise in her cheeks. "Yes," she mumbled.

"Slut."

Mbosa turned to his companions and said something. A brief discussion followed. Then he turned back to Lia.

"You will take us to it."

"If you'll take me with you."

He paused for a second.

"All right, little whore. Now show us."

Lia hesitated for a moment. Then, her wrists still cuffed behind her, she set off. "It's this way."

# Chapter 11

The strange group made its way through the forest, the naked girl, her arms pinned behind her, leading four rough-looking men, her pale body a stark contrast to theirs.

Lia was acutely aware of the sight she made, but somehow it seemed strangely arousing to be as she was, naked in the company of the men.

It took nearly fifteen minutes to retrace the route to the Hispanic's house. All the time her ears were tuned for the sound of motorcycle engines, which would tell her that the Bikers were aware of their escape, but it stayed quiet. At last she glimpsed a glow of light through the trees.

Clearly Mbosa had seen the light too, and brought the group to a stop. He said something to his companions, then moved forward. Lia stood with the other men, wishing she had some way to cover her nakedness.

After about five minutes he returned and had a short discussion with his colleagues. Then he took Lia by the arm and pulled her forward with him.

They stopped beside a bush. In front was an open space of about fifty yards, in the middle of which was parked the car. Beyond was the house. Lia shivered slightly as she caught sight of the three men who had gang-banged her. They were sitting at a table on a low veranda, drinking.

"See the guns," murmured Mbosa.

Lia squinted. Indeed, on the table she could see a pistol, and leaning beside the front door was a rifle.

"If we try to get close they'll see us," said the man. "We will be easy targets. I don't want a gunfight. Too dangerous and too much noise. Biker bastards will hear. You must distract them."

Lia stared at him. "Me?"

He sniffed with contempt. "It is what you are here for," he said.

"What do you want me to do?"

"You go and distract them," he said. "Get them inside, so they don't see us coming."

"But how?"

"You know how, slut. Use your tits and cunt."

Lia felt her cheeks redden. "But I..."

Mbosa grabbed her arm and turned her to face him. "But nothing. You have already shown us how shameless you are. Now get over there and do what you are good at."

He turned the teenager round, and moments later Lia felt her cuffs being undone. She rubbed her wrists, caressing the red marks that the restraints had made.

"Now go, and get them inside."

Lia looked across at the house, and at the three men. Her thoughts went back to her previous encounter with the trio, the rough fucking she had received, the three of them using her then discarding her.

"Turn around."

Lia obeyed, and felt the cuffs being removed from her wrists. Then Mbosa gave her a shove.

"Get them inside, away from the guns," he said. "Now move!"

Lia swallowed hard. Then, her heart fluttering, she stepped out of the cover of the woods and began her walk across to the house. She kept her eyes fixed on the three men. At first they didn't notice her. Then she saw one of them look up, and a shiver ran through her as he nudged the man beside him and pointed at her.

Lia tried to remain calm as she approached, her breasts quivering enticingly with every step. She could hear them laughing, and the blood rose in her cheeks as she considered how she must appear to them; a brazen, naked slut, returning to the men who had gang-banged her such a short time before. Every instinct made her want to turn and run, but she was only too aware of what Mbosa would do if she did.

"Fuck me, you got no clothes on again," sneered one of the men.

"She already told us she likes to fuck," said his companion.

"She likes our cocks, I think," said the third.

Lia tried not to listen to their comments as she approached. She stepped up onto the porch and stopped in front of them. She wanted to cover herself with her hands, but knew that wasn't what Mbosa wanted of her. Instead she let her arms hang at her sides, moving her legs apart so the men would see the wet sheen on her sex lips.

"H-hello," she stammered.

"What the fuck you want?"

"I... I just came to see you again."

"You liked what you got last time?"

"I..."

"Go on, tell us."

Lia's face reddened. "I liked what I got last time."

The men turned to one another and spoke in Spanish for a moment. Lia couldn't understand what they were saying, but their guffaws made it clear they found her situation amusing. Somehow, though, they weren't reacting as she had expected. By now she'd assumed they would be feeling her up, playing with her naked body.

One of the three stood up. "You want to come inside?"

Lia's heart leaped. They were doing exactly what she required. "Yes please," she said.

"You may not like it."

The man's words brought fresh laughter from his companions. She looked at him quizzically, but already he was leading her to the front door. He opened it and pushed her inside.

"What the fuck?"

The voice surprised her. She had expected to find the room empty, but there, sitting in front of a television sat three women, Hispanic, like the men. At the sight of the naked girl being shoved into the room their eyes widened.

"What you doin' Paolo?"

"Remember I told you about that naked slut who came by here last week?"

"This her?"

"Yeah, and she's still looking to get fucked."

One of the women rose to her feet. She was taller than Lia, in her late twenties. There was a scowl on her face that sent a shiver through the young beauty.

"You the bitch who tried to get our guys to fuck you?"

Lia stared at her. "No. I..."

"Sure she did," put in Paolo. "Like I told you, she turned up naked, begging for it. Course we told her to get outta here."

Lia looked at him, staggered by his lying.

The woman moved closer to her. "This true? You came here naked?"

"Yes, but..."

"I told you, she's a sex-mad slut," said Paolo. "You can see she is. Why else would she go around naked, her cunt shaved like that?"

"You come here tonight to get fucked?" asked the woman.

"No. I mean..." Lia's voice trailed away. She couldn't tell them the truth. She couldn't let on that the Hamites were waiting in the trees. She was trapped in Paolo's lies now.

"Did you?"

Lia hung her head. "Yes," she said.

The other two women were on their feet now.

"Fucking whore."

"Stealing our men. What the fuck did you think they'd do with a scrawny little body like yours?"

The two were as tall as the first, and Lia shrank back as they approached her.

"What we gonna do with the little bitch?"

"Show her what we do to women who try to steal our men. Leave her with us, Paolo."

The man grinned. "She's all yours, babes."

Lia watched in alarm as he left the room, returning to his companions. This wasn't going right at all. What would Mbosa think when he saw the three men still outside? Would he think she had betrayed him?

Her more immediate fears came to the fore as the women moved closer.

"Little slut."

"Yeah. Why don't we let everyone know she's a little slut?" said the one who had first confronted her.

"What you mean, Marta?"

She turned to her friends. "She doesn't wear clothes like a decent lady. Why don't we advertise the slut's needs? You still got those marker pens, Paula?"

"The ones that don't wash out? Yeah. But why?"

"Oh, I get it," said the third. "Go get them, Paula."

The woman opened a drawer. Lia watched, puzzled, as she pulled a marker pen out.

"Give it to me," said Marta. "Deb, you and Paula hold the bitch's arms."

Once again Lia took a step backward, but Paula already had hold of her arm, her nails digging into Lia's flesh as she held her. Moments later Deb had hold of her other arm, and the helpless teenager watched fearfully as Marta stepped closer.

She uncapped the pen. Then dropping to one knee, she applied it to Lia's bare stomach, who watched in horror as the word SLUT was written across her belly in large black letters.

"There we are," said Marta. "That says it all."

"Yeah," said Deb. "But why not let the guys know what she wants?"

Marta laughed. "Sure." She applied the pen again, this time lower down.

"No, please," said Lia, but already Marta had written FUCK MY CUNT in clear letters, adding an arrow that pointed down at Lia's bare slit.

"I reckon she likes her tits being felt as well," said Paula.

Marta laughed. Then rising to her feet she scrawled FEEL MY TITS over the top of Lia's lovely breasts.

"You think she takes it up the ass?" asked Deb.

"A shameless whore like this? Course she does. Turn the bitch round."

Lia was turned, presenting her shapely backside to the Hispanic woman. She felt the pen on her rear cheeks.

"I'm writing FUCK MY ASS, bitch," she said.

"Right, let's take a look."

The girls released Lia from their grip and she stood, her cheeks burning as they stared at her, laughing. She could scarcely believe the ignominy of what was happening to her. It was bad enough being forced to be naked in front of them, but to have her body decorated in this awful way was too much. She just wanted to hide from the mocking eyes and comments.

"Right, now we're going to thrash you," said Marta. "Go get a belt, Deb."

"No, please..."

"Shut the fuck up. Paula, you wanna get some duct tape?

"But I..." Lia fell silent as an idea came to her. One that would satisfy Mbosa and might even save her from the ensuing beating.

"P-please, don t let the men see me," she said.

"They already saw you."

"But not like this."

Marta laughed. "Hey, the bitch is right. The guys will enjoy this."

She went across to the door and opened it.

"Hey, boys, come see the whore get thrashed."

Lia heard chairs scraping back. Much as she dreaded being seen like this, she knew she must get the men inside.

"Shit!"

"She really does want it."

"Nice cunt for fucking."

The men's laughter and mocking comments sounded awful to the embarrassed youngster. She stood in front of the men, her arms at her sides, her head hanging down as they examined her graffiti-covered body.

"Okay, bring her over to the table," ordered Marta. "Let's put some colour into those ass cheeks."

Once again Lia felt her arms grasped and was dragged across to a pine table. The women were strong, and her struggles in vain as she was roughly shoved down over the surface, her bare breasts crushed against the cool wood. The women wrapped duct tape about her wrists. She was helpless, her body bent over across the table, her wrists taped to two corners, her bare backside presented perfectly for the thrashing she was to receive. The women kicked her legs apart, and she knew the men had a perfect view of her pussy as she lay helpless.

"Right," said Marta. "Now we'll show you what we do with tarts who try to steal our men."

"Please, I wasn't trying to steal them."

"Shut the fuck up. Give me the belt, Deb."

"Give it to her, Marta."

"Yeah, thrash the whore."

Marta looked down at the naked girl, a cruel grin on her face. Then she drew her arm back.

Whack!

The belt swept down hard across the pale globes of Lia's backside, bringing a yelp of pain from her as it bit into her soft flesh.

Whack!

The woman had extraordinary strength, dragging another cry from the stricken teenager, her bottom painted with two angry stripes.

Whack!

Whack!

Whack!

The woman showed no mercy as she wielded the belt, each blow planting a new stripe across Lia's ass. She was in agony, pulling vainly at her bonds, her body dancing with pain, but there was no way she could avoid the vicious blows.

Whack!

Whack!

Whack!

Lia was crying for mercy as the belt cut again and again into her flesh. She had broken out in a sheen of sweat and the tears were pouring down her cheeks.

Whack!

Whack!

Whack...!

With a loud crash the front door flew open.

"Everyone stand still!"

Mbosa stood in the doorway brandishing his pistol. Behind were his companions, holding the guns that had been outside. The three men and women stood, their faces frozen in shock, as Mbosa strode into the room. He glanced down at Lia, his eyes taking in the cruel red stripes that decorated her bottom.

"I reckon she deserved that," he said, with a faint grin.

# Chapter 12

By the time the Hamites turned their attention to Lia the six occupants of the house had been taken care of. Their wrists and ankles bound with the duct tape they lay on the floor, clearly bemused by what had happened to them.

Once satisfied they were in control the four men began to move about the house, taking food and liquor as they found it, loading it into boxes and placing them in the car. All this time Lia was left where she was. Only when the men were ready to leave did Mbosa go to where she lay bound to the table.

"You still wanna come with us?"

"Yes please."

He gave a sniff of disdain, then picked up a sharp knife that lay near the trapped girl. He began to slice through Lia's bonds, the knife making short work of the tape. When he slit through the last piece of tape the girl was able to straighten up, reaching back and gingerly rubbing her sore backside.

Mbosa let out a sudden laugh. Lia stared at him for a moment, uncertain what was amusing him. Then her eyes dropped to her naked body and the blood rose in her cheeks as she remembered the awful words scrawled across her skin.

"I guess these people saw you for what you are," he said, tracing the word SLUT with his fingers.

His three companions gathered around her.

"Babe says she needs a fuck."

"I'll feel those pretty tits, honey."

"I-I need to wash," she stammered.

"Ha! Doesn't look like that'll wash off in a hurry," mocked Walagu.

"Anyhow, no time for that," said Mbosa. "We gotta get out of her. Get out to the car." He gave Lia a shove towards the door.

Outside, he climbed into the driving seat while Lia was bundled into the rear between Walagu and one of the others. The engine sprang into life and they pulled away from the rundown building.

As they reached the track the car surged forward, the speed increasing. Lia felt somewhat nervous as she watched the trees flash past, but Mbosa drove with skill, the car speeding through the woods. He took a turn, heading away from where she knew the town to be, and she wondered where they were going. He was clearly driving with purpose.

She felt a hand on her leg. She turned to see Walagu staring at her naked body, his hand running slowly up her thigh. Instinctively she pressed her knees together.

"You don't give yourself to black men?" he said.

"I don't want to."

"You don't fuck with Hamites? Just with white trash?"

"No. I just mean... Please, I..."

He moved his hand further up her thigh. "You have been fucked before, haven't you?"

Lia felt the blood rise in her cheeks. "Yes, but..."

"Tell us about it."

"No, please."

"Come on, you can tell us. By how many men have you been fucked?"

"I don't know."

"One? Two? Five?"

"I don't know."

"A hundred?"

"I don't know."

"It could be more than that?"

Lia's cheeks glowed. She really didn't know how many men had fucked her. She didn't even know the names of most of them. In her early time as a slave of the Bikers she had been used almost daily. Particularly when she had been a naked hostess at The Black Cat, Helda's sex club.

A second hand was on her. The man sitting on her other side. Lia bit her lip as his fingers closed over her breast, making the nipple harden at once.

"Please..."

"But you like it," said the man. Look, Walagu, how her nipple grows hard."

Walagu grinned. "You're right, Ngorah. He moved his hand up and began caressing Lia's other breast.

She sat between the two men, her mind in a whirl. They were strong and masculine, with the calloused hands of manual workers, and the sensation of having her breasts roughly caressed by them was bringing unwelcome sensations within her. Already she could feel the moisture leaking from her vagina, and she gritted her teeth, hating the perverse way her body responded to the touch of the men.

"Spread your legs."

"N-no. Please."

"Fucking spread them, babe. You know you want to."

Lia looked at Walagu. His gaze was intent, and she felt an odd feeling in her stomach as he took in her body. She bit her lip. Then she moved her legs apart.

A smile played on Walagu's lips as he saw she was compliant. He moved his hand down to her leg again, stroking the smooth flesh.

Lia sat still, her heart thumping as the two men toyed with her, the one called Ngorah caressing her bare breasts while Walagu's fingers crept higher up her inner thigh. In the mirror she could see Mbosa's eyes occasionally straying in her direction. The man beside him was turned in his seat, watching as the two caressed her naked flesh, a smile on his lips.

"Oh!" Lia gave an involuntary cry as Walagu's fingers found her vagina. He slipped a finger into her, bringing a groan from her.

"Your cunt's wet," he remarked. You like to have a man's fingers inside you?"

"I... no, I just... ah!" Once again a cry escaped her lips as a finger began to toy with her clitoris. She could feel the bud of flesh harden under his touch and her hips began to gyrate as he shoved his digits deeper into the heat and wetness of her vagina.

Then a hand was grabbing her hair, pulling her head down. Lia's eyes widened as she saw Ngorah had opened his fly. His cock stood proud from his jeans, like a stiff black rod.

"You like to eat cock, don't you?"

Lia eyed the rigid pole. She could smell his maleness, the scent bringing a new shiver of excitement to her.

"You want to taste it?"

"I..."

"Sure you do. Take it, whore."

He pressed her down to it. Lia opened her mouth.

"That's it," he said as he pushed her face into his groin.

Lia closed her lips about his penis, squeezing them around the thick rod, taking the shaft in her hand. The scent of male arousal was all around her now, and she found herself sucking greedily at his massive erection, the fingers inside her sex sending new thrills of pleasure through her body.

"Get up on the seat," said Walagu. "On all fours."

It was an order. One she was expected to obey. Keeping Ngorah's cock between her lips she complied, scrambling up onto the seat, her head buried between the black man's thighs.

She felt Walagu's fingers explore her sex from behind, pressing deep unto her love tunnel, causing a new flow of wetness as he fingered her. She wondered at the sight she was giving him, her legs spread, her anus and vagina on open view to him. Somehow the thought brought a new thrill to the perverse girl and she thrust her bottom back at him, continuing to suck the cock in her mouth.

When she felt a stiff penis nudging against her bum a new shudder of arousal ran through her. Whilst continuing to service Ngorah's rampant erection with her hand and mouth she reached the other back, closing it about the throbbing stiffness of Walagu's penis.

"You want it now," said the man.

Lia's response was to guide his gland to the wetness of her sex. She was losing control, and her behaviour was making it clear to the gang that they could use her as they wanted, but she knew they would anyway, whether she liked it or not.

"Mmmmph!"

The cock in her mouth muffled her cry as Walagu began pressing his cock into her vagina, taking her to a new level of excitement, pushing back against him, urging him deeper. Walagu required no more encouragement, ramming his cock into her until he filled her totally. Then he began to fuck her hard.

Lia's body was driven back and forth, her breasts trembling deliciously as she responded to the men's actions. She should be protesting, but the taste of male arousal along with the intense pleasure of having a thick cock rammed into her, left her gasping with desire.

Ngorah's thrusts were becoming more urgent, his hand gripping her hair as he forced his penis deep into her throat. Lia responded by sucking harder, her tongue lapping his glans while her fist pumped his stout cock.

He gave a grunt, and Lia's mouth filled with spunk. The cock twitched violently as it pumped load after load of salty fluid into her mouth. Lia sucked greedily, obediently swallowing his sperm.

A gasp from Walagu told her that he too had reached his climax. Moments later more thick spunk erupted into the gasping teenager, bringing her to an extraordinary orgasm, her backside jerking back and forth as she revelled in the fucking she was getting.

Ngorah withdrew his penis from her mouth, a trickle of sperm running from her lips down to her chin. Walagu went on grinding, emptying his balls into her pulsating vagina.

Then, at last, he was done, his motions slowing as the moaning girl slumped forward, her face red with exertion.

Mbosa glanced back in the mirror at the two weary men and the gasping teenager, then turned to the man next to him.

"You want to fuck her, Legani?"

"Yeah. Stop the car and let me get in the back."

# Chapter 13

Lia opened her eyes, blinking the sleep from them as something alerted her. She looked about, but could see nothing since she was surrounded by darkness. She reached out and felt a cardboard box beside her. She was lying on some kind of rough mat that chafed her flesh. With a sinking feeling she realized she was still naked. But where was she?

It began to come back to her, and she remembered the escape and where she was. She was lying in the trunk of the stolen car.

She reached between her legs and felt the spunk seeping from her vagina. She remembered Legani climbing into the back of the car, making her straddle his lap. He fucked her, then no sooner had he come than Ngorah and Walagu fucked her again. She remembered her own reaction, the number of shattering orgasms that had engulfed her in the hands of the rough gang.

She did not know how far they had gone when Mbosa pulled over by a public telephone. He said a few words to the others, then climbed out.

While he was on the phone she was lifted from the rear seat. Ignoring her protests they unceremoniously dumped her into the trunk of the car, and slammed it shut.

She wondered at the time why Mbosa had not used her naked body. She remembered the expression of contempt on his face as he watched her in the mirror and listened to her shameful moans of passion. Clearly he had an extremely low opinion of her.

The car had stopped. But where were they? She strained to hear anything that would give her a clue, but in vain.

Then there was the sound of a key in the trunk and it sprang open. She found herself staring up at Mbosa.

"Get out," he said.

Lia scrambled out, the ground cold under her bare feet, and she shivered as she stood in front of her captors.

"In there. Get moving."

Lia looked in the direction Mbosa was pointing, and her heart sank. It was a rundown building, the windows dirty, the paint peeling, a red-lit *Bar* sign over the door.

She had seen such places before, but had never been inside one. It was an establishment owned and run by Hamites. Many of the bars and restaurants had segregation policies and would not serve the Hamites, so they responded by opening their own places, usually in the poor areas where they lived. Never had she thought she might enter one, and certainly not in her current state.

"Could I have something to wear?" she asked.

"Just get the fuck inside. And fast; we don't want to be seen with you out here." Mbosa shoved her forward. "Inside!"

Lia began to walk towards the entrance of the bar.

"Not in there. The side entrance."

She saw a door to one side, and headed towards it. Ngorah pulled the door, which opened with a creak. She stepped inside, looking about nervously. She was in a short corridor lit by a bare lightbulb, the paint on the walls stained and old. The men followed her.

"In there," said Mbosa.

He pointed to a door with *Office* on it in faded letters. Her heart beating hard, Lia turned the handle and pushed it open.

A somewhat overweight black man sat behind a desk. He wore a check suit with wide lapels that looked gaudy and cheap, as did his tie. Between his lips was a thick cigar. Lia shrank back under his gaze, but was pushed forward by Mbosa as the others entered.

The man rose and held out a hand. Mbosa shook it, his face expressionless. Then the man turned and looked the naked girl up and down.

"Say, the bitch ain't bad," he said. "She always go about like this?"

"Cheap little slut," said Mbosa.

"You guys been fucking her?"

Ngorah let out a grunt of laughter. "Sure. It's what she wants."

Lia tried to closer her ears to the remarks, looking about the small office. Like the corridor the walls needed a coat of paint. Aside from the old desk there were some tatty chairs. On a shelf was a monitor, and on it she could see the flickering black and white images of men drinking in a bar. This bar, she assumed, and the man was the owner or manager.

"Bitch needs cleaning up," he said. With a thumb he pointed over his shoulder to a door behind him. "Bathroom through there."

Mbosa glanced at Lia, then nodded. "Two minutes," he said.

Lia moved across the room, pulling open the door. There was a switch on the wall and she flicked it, bathing the room in light. It was a small bathroom, with a toilet and a sink, a mirror on the wall. She pushed the door shut, then glanced in the mirror. At once her heart sank.

She gazed at the writing scrawled across her naked flesh, emblazoned there for all to see, her backside provocatively daubed in a similar manner.

She glanced down at the sink. There wasn't even a bar of soap. She tore off a wad of toilet paper, ran it under the tap and wiped hard at the letters, but with no effect.

"Get a move on!"

She gazed down at her thighs, which were streaked with semen. She bent and began to wipe the stains from her flesh, running the wad up her thighs. It took some time before she was reasonably clean. Then she flushed away the paper and, taking a deep breath, made her way back into the room.

The men were deep in discussion, seated around the desk. Mbosa seemed to be doing most of the talking, the tone of his voice rising occasionally. It was clear to Lia that the men were bargaining, but she understood nothing of what was being said. She noticed that Mbosa was gesturing towards her occasionally, and that the man behind the desk was constantly eyeing her.

Her eyes drifted to the monitor and the drinking men.

"You fancy a beer?"

Lia jumped, tearing her eyes from the screen.

Mbosa was looking at her. "You like to drink in bars?"

"I... I was just looking."

"Maybe you could show Sagana here how you love to be naked with men."

Lia stared at him, not understanding what he was talking about. Mbosa turned back to the manager and suggested something. Smiles broke out all round and the manager nodded.

"Get over here, girl."

Warily Lia made her way to the desk, not at all liking the way the man was eyeing her.

"This is Sagana," said Mbosa. "He is interested in looking after you."

"I don't understand."

"When we leave."

"But aren't I going with you?"

Mbosa shook his head. "No. We can't keep you with us. The sight of three black men with a white girl is too conspicuous. We'd get picked up by the Bikers in no time."

Lia was taken aback. Much as she feared Mbosa and his men, she felt a certain allegiance to them; they hated the Bikers, after all.

"Sagana won't keep you. No, I have a use for you. But for now you'll stay with him."

"If he'll have her," put in Ngorah.

Mbosa allowed himself a slight smile. "Yes. He wants to put you to the test. To check your obedience."

"I don't understand."

Mbosa turned to the man behind the desk. "Tell her."

Sagana sat back in his chair, his eyes fixed on Lia's naked form.

"These men tell me you will give your body willingly," he said. "Is that true?"

Lia felt her cheeks redden. "I... I sometimes let men have me," she stammered.

Walagu laughed. "She gave herself to us willingly enough," he said. "And she enjoyed it."

Lia cast her eyes down, saying nothing.

"Well," said Sagana. "We're going to see. I want you to go get yourself a beer."

"A beer?"

"Yes." He opened the drawer on his desk and pulled out a bill. "Take this and go buy yourself a beer. Just act like an ordinary customer. If anyone in there wants anything from you, then give it."

"Anything?"

"Anything."

"But they might want...'

"To fuck you? So what?"

Lia glanced up at the screen, and a shiver ran through her.

"Please. I..."

"Get a move on," said Sagana. "Go in the front door like any other customer We'll be watching."

Lia stared round at the five men, then down at her naked flesh still daubed with the dreadful writing.

Ngorah moved across to the door, which he opened. "Go."

# Chapter 14

As Lia stepped out of the scruffy corridor into the bar's car park she was almost shaking with fearful anticipation. Walking into a strange bar naked, with shameful words emblazoning her skin, was almost unthinkable.

She looked about. The neighbourhood was quiet. Perhaps she could make her escape. Perhaps she could make a run for it.

The idea died as quickly as it had come to her. Naked and alone in this area was a worse prospect than being in the hands of Mbosa and his friends. She was a fugitive now, sought by the Bikers. She had to go along with Mbosa or risk falling into their hands.

She stopped just outside the bar, staring at the peeling paint on the door. She glanced down, her eyes taking in her jutting breasts, the nipples hard and upstanding. She could already feel the wetness inside her vagina as her body reacted to her situation, and that wetness would soon be visible. She reached down and found her clitoris, her finger running over the little bud, sending shudders of perverse arousal through her. Then, taking a deep breath, she stepped forward, pushing the door open and walking inside.

She saw the bar in front of her. There were three men sitting on stools, and a number of others at tables around the room. Soft music was playing from speakers on the wall. The lights were brighter than she would have liked, her pale skin in stark contrast to the scruffy patrons.

For a moment nobody looked in her direction. Then she saw one of the men at the bar nudge his companion and point in her direction. She saw his eyebrows rise, and a smile form on his lips. Then a murmur went up as more eyes turned in her direction until she was the centre of attention.

She padded across to the bar, aware that the talking had stopped as the men watched her. She tried not to think of the sight she made.

Behind the bar was a black woman, overweight and grim-faced. At the sight of the naked teenager her eyes widened. Lia was overwhelmed by shame. More than anything else she wanted to turn and run, but she dare not. Feeling the blood flowing into her cheeks, she stopped at the bar.

"What the..." said the woman.

"I'd like a beer, please."

"Where your clothes?"

"I... I'm not wearing any."

"I can see that. What's your game?"

"I just want a beer, please."

"You can't just come in here like that and expect to get served."

"Please. I just want a beer."

The woman's eyes dropped to Lia's breasts and her face creased into a frown.

"What's that writing for? She said, pointing at Lia's breasts.

"It's nothing," stammered the girl.

"That ain't nothing. Tell me what it says."

"You can see."

"Tell me."

"It... it says feel my tits."

"You some kind of sex freak?"

"I just want a beer, please."

The woman tut-tutted, shaking her head. Then she pulled a bottle of beer from a fridge and opened it, handing it to Lia. Her face still crimson, the naked youngster took a swig of the cool liquid.

She looked about. The bar clearly hadn't been decorated for some years, the paintwork stained from tobacco smoke, the carpet worn and dotted with cigarette burns. It was not the sort of place she would normally enter, even if she was decently dressed. To be standing in it naked was almost unthinkable.

"Hey babe. That really what you want?"

She turned to the man standing next to her at the bar. He was middle-aged, wearing a tattered jacket and stained trousers. His eyes were fixed on her

68

breasts, a leer on his face.

"I beg your pardon?"

"You want me to feel your tits?"

She said nothing, her cheeks glowing.

"That's what you wrote there, isn't it?"

"I-I didn't write it."

"You didn't cover it up either. Come here."

Nervously she moved closer to the man, making his grin widen.

"That's good."

He reached out a hand, making Lia instinctively shy away.

"C'mon babe."

She stood, her hands at her sides as he reached out again, closing his hand over her breast, pinching the nipple, teasing it between finger and thumb. At once the dark bud hardened, a fact that was not lost on the man.

"See, you like it."

Lia drew back, but standing close to the bar she couldn't get away from the man, who moved closer, his eyes still fixed on her breasts. His body was against hers now, and she shuddered as she felt the hardness of his crotch pressing against her tummy.

He had both hands on her breasts now, caressing the soft flesh, teasing her nipples into erectness as her recalcitrant body responded to his touch. Lia bit her lip, aware that the other patrons were watching. Aware too that Mbosa and Sagana would be studying her reactions from the office. Her instinct told her to push the drunk away, but she dare not, so she stood, hands by her sides while he mauled her.

"Turn around, baby. Turn around. I wanna read what's on that pretty little ass."

"Please..."

"Turn around."

Reluctantly she did as he said.

"It says *fuck my ass*. You like being fucked in the ass?"

"No. I just..."

"That's what it says here." His fingers traced the words written there. "Fuck my ass. That looks like a pretty clear invitation to me."

He ran his hand over Lia's beautiful buttocks, then slid his fingers down the crack, seeking out her tight little anus. She drew in her breath as she felt his finger press against her nether hole.

"Bend over. Let me feel it properly."

"Please, I..."

He placed his hand on her back, pushing. "Bend over."

Reluctantly she bent over the bar stool in front of her, her cheeks glowing as she considered the sight she made.

"Open your legs."

"Look, couldn't we...?"

Whack! A hand swatted Lia's naked backside, making her squeal with pain.

"Just fucking open them."

Slowly she moved her legs apart.

"Very nice. What you think, Lumba?"

Another man moved around to share his companion's view.

"Yeah. Sure is a pretty asshole."

"And she's asking for it to be fucked."

"Could I stand up now?" Lia was acutely embarrassed by the sight she was making. Every fibre of her being desired to get out of the awful bar, and to cover her body.

"No, stay like that."

"Oh!" She gave a start as she felt a finger penetrate her anus. Her instinct was to push it away, but she daren't. Instead she gritted her teeth as the man explored.

"You gonna give it to her?" asked the other one.

"Sure. Gotta keep the lady happy. Hey, Petal, can we use the pool room?"

"What for?" asked the barmaid.

"Give this young lady a bit of privacy."

The woman looked at Lia, her face a picture of disdain. "Sure. Just don't make a mess."

"C'mon, baby, we're gonna give you what you want."

Lia felt the finger removed from her behind. She was pulled upright and the two men took her across the room to another door.

She tried to close her ears to the coarse and humiliating comments of the other customers as she was led into the pool room. It was small, and as scruffy as the bar. There was a single pool table in the middle of the floor, over to which she was led.

"Right, bend forward and spread your legs."

Lia looked at the two men, a protest springing to her lips. Then her shoulders slumped. She knew she had no control over what would happen. Slowly, reluctantly, she turned round and faced the table. Then, placing her hands on the cloth she bent forward, moving her legs apart.

"That's good."

The first man moved behind her. Lia stiffened as she felt his hands on her backside again, squeezing and caressing the soft flesh. Then a hand slipped lower, between her legs, and she barely suppressed a gasp as she felt his fingers slip into her vagina.

"Shit, she's hot and wet," he said to his companion.

"Bitch wants it bad."

The words brought new shame to her as she realized her body was reacting to the sordid treatment in an unwanted way, her nipples stiffening, her sex exuding a warm wetness as the man caressed it.

He took hold of her hand, pulling it back to his crotch. His flies were undone. He guided her hand inside and she felt the hardness of his cock as it strained against his underpants. Almost automatically she found herself fumbling inside those pants, her fingers closing around his erection as she freed it.

"That's it, babe. You like the feel of a black cock, don't you?"

Lia said nothing, but her hand caressed his penis, feeling it becoming harder and thicker.

The man leant forward, and Lia felt a wetness on her anus. He had spat on her, rubbing the saliva into her tight nether hole. Then he shuffled closer and she felt the glans pressing against her rear entrance.

"Relax, baby. You know you want it."

He pushed her hand away and, taking his shaft in his own fist, began pressing against her nether hole. Lia's natural reaction was to tighten her muscles to keep him out, but she knew it would do no good. Closing her eyes tight she leant forward against the pool table and tried her best to relax her sphincter as he pressed harder.

"Ah!" Lia cried as his cock penetrated her rear. She bit her lip at the discomfort as he pressed on, his penis slipping deeper and deeper until it filled her rectum.

"There, babe. All the way in," he croaked.

"And you're loving it," put in his companion.

He began to fuck her asshole, gently at first, his hips pumping his rampant cock back and forth. For Lia it was an extraordinary sensation, and she felt a trickle of wetness leak onto her thigh as her body reacted to the humiliating treatment. There was an extraordinary intensity to being fucked this way, and she found her excitement rising as he continued to take his pleasure in her.

His hips were pumping harder now as he gripped her hips, ramming his hefty erection into her anus, his breath coming in grunts as his arousal increased. His companion watched, spellbound, as his friend buggered the beautiful girl.

Lia clung to the table, her body shaken with every thrust, her breasts shuddering deliciously as the man's passions continued to excite her. She wanted to reach down and caress her swollen clitoris, to bring her some of the pleasure the man was experiencing, but his pounding was too aggressive and she dare not take a hand from the supporting table.

His grip on her was tightening, and she could sense he was approaching his climax. Then he was coming, his breath rasping as he pumped hot spunk into Lia's rectum. She responded by pressing back, as if urging him to penetrate even deeper, the sensation of his seed pouring into her bringing her an extraordinary thrill. She wished she could have an orgasm, her arousal overriding all discomfort and humiliation as she experienced a stiff cock shooting its load into her rear passage.

He continued to fuck her ass, his thrusts decreasing as his passion slowly drained until at last he was done. Lia gritted her teeth as she felt his erection withdraw from her anus, a trickle of spunk leaking onto her thigh.

Before she was able to catch her breath she felt her arm grabbed by the other man, and she was pressed down on her back on the stained carpet

71

Lia gazed up at him. He had undone his trousers and his cock stood proudly from them. Despite her shame she knew it was what she needed, and she moved he legs apart, presenting him with perfect access to her sex.

He required no further invitation. Dropping to his knees he fell forward over her body. His cock pressing against her pussy lips.

Lia gave a cry of passion as he entered her, shoving his cock deep into her vagina. It felt good to be filled so completely, and the walls of her sex contracted about his penis, her hips pressing up against his. She writhed under him, her cries of excitement echoing about the room. Her brain was telling her to protest, but her body was betraying her once more, her sex weeping fluid as the hefty cock speared into her.

The man grinned as he gazed down at her naked, ravaged body, her breasts shaking, her nipples hard as he mauled them with rough hands.

"You ready for another helping of spunk?" he growled as his thrusts increased. "Sure you are, you sexy little whore."

As she felt her vagina filling with spunk Lia came too, her hips jabbing up as she cried out with lust. The climax was an exquisite one, the man keeping his erection buried deep as her orgasm overcame her.

Lia gave an involuntary moan as she felt him withdraw. Moments later his cock was in her face as he told her to lick him clean. Lia took him into her mouth, tasting his spunk and her own fluids, her hips continuing to gyrate as her orgasm slowly ebbed.

Once satisfied the man rose to his feet, tucking his cock back into his pants. Then he pulled the naked girl back to her feet.

"C'mon, slut," he said. "You ain't finished your beer yet."

# Chapter 15

Lia braced herself as the car bumped along, wondering where she was headed for now. Once again she was surrounded by darkness, lying on a rough carpet. This was a different car trunk, but no more comfortable than the last one.

Still, it was a relief to be away from the lustful gazes of the men in the rough saloon. When they'd finished with her the two men took her back into the bar. Again her embarrassment was acute as she entered the room naked. This time her condition was even more discomforting, as her anus and sex were leaking spunk that she knew was clearly visible to the onlookers. Even had her recent sexual encounter not been obvious, the men were boasting about their conquest with much enthusiasm.

They took Lia to the bar, where she was obliged to finish her beer under the fixed gazes of the other customers. She had felt extremely uncomfortable standing there, her breasts on open display, the nipples hard. The customers were talking about her, laughing at her promiscuity and she knew that, at any moment, she might be called upon again to surrender to one or more of them. So it was almost with relief that she saw Sagana appear from a door and beckon to her. She made her way across to where he was standing, noting the smile on his lips as he took in her state.

"You have been fucked, I see."

Lia blushed. "Yes Sir."

"And they brought you to orgasm?"

"Yes Sir."

He shook his head, then motioned towards the door. "Get in there."

Lia obeyed, pushing the door open amid the laughter and cheers of the men.

She found herself outside the office. The door opened and Mbosa and his three colleagues came out.

"You seemed to enjoy that," Mbosa said.

Obviously there had been another camera in the pool room, and they'd witnessed everything. She said nothing, her cheeks glowing with shame.

"I will be back for you," Mbosa went on. "I have plans for a brazen one like you. For now you must obey Sagana. Remember, it would be very easy to dump you outside a Biker hangout and let you take what's coming to you. The Bikers have a low opinion of women who mix with Hamites."

He turned and followed his companions out through the door. Lia watched them, turning over in her mind what he had said. What plans could he possibly have for her? A shiver went through her as she turned to face Sagana.

"Right," he said, "get out to my car."

So here she was, bumping along in the trunk of Sagana's rusting old gas guzzler, wondering anxiously what fate had in store for her next.

They drove for about ten minutes. The car seemed to be going fast and Lia was forced to hang on to whatever she could as she listened to the tires screech through the corners. Then the road became rougher, the bouncing vehicle almost knocking the breath out of the youngster as they sped along. At last there was a final swing to the left, and the engine died. A few moments later the trunk lid opened, and Lia found herself staring up at Sagana.

"Get out," he ordered.

Lia hurried to obey, glad to be out of the stuffy trunk. She climbed out, then glanced about. They were in a quiet wooded spot, outside a house in a similar state to the bar, its paint peeling, the windows dirty.

"Listen to me."

She turned to face Sagana.

"You're gonna be here for a while," said the man. "While you're here you're gonna be my servant. Savvy?"

"Y-yes."

"Yes Sir."

"Yes Sir."

"Good. Now you don't want people to know you're on the run from the Bikers, do you?"

"No Sir."

"Right. So it'll be in your interest to say you're here willingly. That you want

73

to be my servant. Right?"

"Yes Sir."

"And you'll willingly do what I tell you to."

"What must I do, Sir?"

"I'll be calling on you to use that pretty little body to amuse my friends."

"Sir?"

"Like you amused those two guys in the bar. You sure seemed to be enjoying it."

Lia's eyes widened. "But I..."

"But nothing. You want to do what I ask of you. That's why you want to be naked right now. Understand?"

"I... yes, Sir."

"So you'll obey me and my housekeeper?"

"H-housekeeper?"

"Sure. Mistress Ikwo will be your boss. You'll obey her like you obey me. Understand?"

"Yes Sir."

Lia pondered these orders. Sagana was right; the fewer people who knew she was on the run, the better. News could travel fast and, even in this remote spot, she was still in danger of being recognized. At the same time, being a servant to the man wasn't exactly what she'd choose - but what choice did she have? Her shoulders slumped. She had escaped the enslavement of the Bikers, but for what?

"Come on. Into the house."

She padded along behind the heavy black man, her eyes taking in the house. It was a large place, with an upstairs and dormer windows in the roof. At the front was a wide veranda, and it was up the steps onto it she was led. The wood felt rough beneath her bare feet as she made her way to the front door.

"Open it for me, servant."

Lia pulled open the door and stood back while he went inside. Then she followed him in.

The hall had a worn carpet, the paintwork, though faded, giving a homely air to the building. A bright light hung from the ceiling, making the naked girl feel even more exposed in its glare.

"Mistress Ikwo!"

From the back of the house footsteps sounded. Lia stood nervously, only too aware of her lack of clothing, and of the filthy words scrawled on her naked flesh.

The door opened and a black woman entered. She was about fifty years old, Lia calculated, a stocky figure wearing a gray dress. She had a time-worn face, and when she saw Lia an expression of surprise crossed her features, quickly followed by one of disgust.

"Who this, Mister Sagana?"

"Her name is not important. She will answer to Girl."

"What's she doing like that?"

"I found her selling her body in my bar."

The woman shook her head, tut-tutting as her eyes took in Lia's condition.

"Look like she made the sale," she said, gazing down at the semen stains on Lia's thighs.

"She has no home, and no belongings. I offered her a job as servant here."

The woman shrugged. "I could use the help," she said. "Where are the slut's clothes?"

"She doesn't have any. It doesn't seem to bother her."

The woman eyed Lia up and down. "You don't mind being naked?"

Lia glanced across at Sagana, who gave a slight nod. She let her eyes drop. "I like to be naked," she said quietly.

The housekeeper shook her head again. "Have you no shame?"

Lia said nothing.

"All right," said the woman. You'd better clean off. And get that disgusting writing off you. There's a bathroom out back of the kitchen. In the cupboard you'll find some stuff to clean yourself good and proper. Go on, get moving."

Lia hurried out through the door the woman was pointing to. It led to a kitchen. The appliances were old and the furniture had seen better days, but it was clean. At the far side was a door, and she went through it. She found herself in a tiled bathroom, with a toilet and shower. She went to the cupboard under the sink and, after rummaging around, found a bottle containing some sort of spirit. Then she set about cleaning herself up.

It was fully twenty minutes before she emerged. She had carefully removed the lettering, then taken a shower. The water was barely warm, but she was only too grateful to wash the evidence of five men from her body. She had found a bottle of shampoo, which allowed her to wash the grime from her hair too. When finished she paused for a moment before the mirror. She felt much better.

Not sure where to go next, she made her way back into the kitchen. Mistress Ikwo was sitting at the table drinking beer. She eyed the youngster up and down.

"Well, at least you're clean, girl," she said. "Come, I'll take you to your room."

She led the way up a wooden staircase, then another, up into the roof. The corridor was narrow, lit by a bare bulb. At the end was a small door.

"In there," said the woman.

Lia stepped inside. It was a tiny room. The wall on one side sloped inward, and the small dormer window had bars across it. The bed was narrow, with a thin grey mattress. There was no other furnishing.

"Get some sleep," said the woman. "There'll be work to do tomorrow."

She closed the door and Lia heard a key turn in the lock.

# Chapter 16

Lia was woken next morning by a banging on her door. She opened her eyes, groggily looking about, temporarily disoriented as she struggled to recall the previous day. It came back to her, and her tummy sank as she realized she was a virtual captive in a strange place.

The key turned in the lock and the blinking youngster recognized the housekeeper staring down at her. She had been allowed no bedclothes, and she found herself curling into a foetal position to hide her nakedness from the woman.

"Get up, girl. The bathroom is at the end of the corridor. Then put this on."

She handed Lia a thin dress. "Just be grateful I'm letting you cover yourself," she said. "Although from what I've seen you enjoy going around like that."

Lia felt her cheeks redden as the woman cast an eye over her nakedness.

"Now get a move on. I want you in the kitchen in ten minutes."

With that she was gone, leaving the teenager to make her way along the dingy corridor.

Ten minutes later she was making her way downstairs, having showered, cleaned her teeth and used the ablutions. On the first landing a mirror hung on the wall, and she paused to glance at her reflection. The dress was indeed small, the thin material clinging tightly to her. The front was cut in a V that dropped almost to her navel, accentuating the swell of her breasts, her nipples standing out clearly. The skirt was so short it barely covered her naked pubic mound, and if she bent forward, even a little, her lack of underwear was obvious. Taking a final glance in the mirror, she continued down the stairs.

In the kitchen Mistress Ikwo was working at the stove. She eyed Lia up and down. "That dress is indecent. I told Mister Sagana, but he wouldn't listen. Said you'd picked it out, and you wanted to wear it. I suppose it suits a shameless little slut like you."

Lia said nothing, her eyes cast down.

"Still, it's time you made yourself useful." The woman indicated a pile of dirty dishes by the sink. "Get to work washing those," she ordered. "And make sure they're clean."

Lia began the washing-up. It wasn't as if she minded being given work. In fact it helped take her mind off her situation. What bothered her was the strangeness of the place, and the humiliation of being kept almost naked. Still, she tried to close her mind to that part of her situation as she set about the dishes, leaning forward over the sink, her breasts quivering and getting splashed as she worked.

When the dishes were done she was allowed a bowl of gruel for breakfast. It was hot and wholesome and she gulped it down, followed by a strong cup of coffee. Then there was more washing and cleaning to be done, as the woman made her scrub all the surfaces in the kitchen until they were spotless.

Mistress Ikwo then gave Lia more chores about the kitchen and its adjoining bathroom, and the youngster worked assiduously, grateful for something to occupy her thoughts and put her precarious situation to the back of her mind. The woman came by frequently, casting a critical eye over her work. Lia could tell she was contemptuous of her. She thought of Lia as a cheap slut, and she couldn't do anything to rid her of that opinion. Still, she did her best to perform her tasks well.

Mid-morning Lia heard the doorbell ring. Her heart sank as she thought of someone else seeing her, and she listened hard as Mistress Ikwo went to the door. The voice she heard was a male one, and she shrank away into the bathroom as she heard the housekeeper talking to whoever it was. She heard the man being taken upstairs, and shortly afterwards the woman descended alone.

It was about an hour later when Mistress Ikwo approached her again. "Go clean up Mister Sagana's bedroom," she ordered. "It's upstairs. Make the bed, dust and sweep up. Get moving."

Lia collected broom and dusters and made for the stairs. As she reached the top she encountered the mirror again, her slutty reflection bringing a new flush of embarrassment. She looked about. There were three doors leading off the landing. Mistress Ikwo hadn't told her which one was the bedroom. She would have to find it for herself.

She opened the first door and looked into the room. It was clearly an office, with a desk and telephone and filing cabinets. She closed the door and went to the second. This time she found a bedroom. The bed was made and had not been slept in. It seemed reasonably neat and tidy, so she guessed it was not the room she'd been sent to clean. But still, to be sure, she bent down to check under the bed for dust.

"Well, what have we here?"

The voice made her jump and she straightened at once, pulling her dress down as best she could over the pert mounds of her backside. The voice came from behind her, and she knew, bending over as she had been, she'd presented whoever it was with a perfect view of her bottom. She turned, then shrank back as she saw the man.

He was a Hamite, in his early twenties she guessed, with wide eyes and a broad grin. He was crouching down by the air conditioner, a screwdriver in his hand, almost hidden by the bed. He rose to his feet, his gaze taking in Lia's scantily clad body, his eyes traveling over her pert breasts and dropping down to where her denuded pubic mound was barely covered by the dress.

"You looking for something?" he asked.

"I-I'm in the wrong room," stammered Lia, backing away.

"From what I'm seeing you're in the right room."

"I have to work." She backed towards the door.

"Don't go," said the man. "You look like you're ready for some fun "

"N-no," she babbled. "I've got things to do."

She fled from the room, closing the door behind her. In the corridor she stopped, trying to regain her composure. What must he thought of her, seeing her like that? She glanced back at the door. Might he come after her? She hurried across to the third door and swung it open, darting inside, relieved to find what was probably Mister Sagana's room, the bed unmade, a cigar butt in the ashtray.

Lia closed the door and immediately set to work, glad of something to take her mind off the recent encounter.

She finished making the bed and was about to start dusting when the door opened. She looked up anxiously, but to her relief the housekeeper entered the room.

"I have to go out for half an hour," said the stern woman. "Make sure this room is spotless when I get back."

"Yes, Ma'am." Lia set to work with the duster. It felt odd doing housework in the skimpy dress. She tried to blot from her mind the sight she must make as she worked, yet even in the dull bedroom she couldn't help feeling oddly aroused by her situation.

"You have a nice ass, baby."

Lia hadn't heard the door opening. She was bent forward over a low table, her back to the door, so she knew she again presented quite a sight to the young man. She swung around, holding the duster in front of her whilst trying to hide the swell of her breasts with her arm. "Wh-what do you want?"

"I just want another look at the sexy white girl. You like that dress?"

"I'm Mister Sagana's servant."

"And he don't let you wear decent clothes?"

"I'm wearing decent clothes." Lia was only too aware that this was not true, but she heeded Sagana's warnings about letting people know she was on the run from the Bikers.

"Why you not wearing underclothes?"

"I... I don't want to."

"So you do like being like that?"

"I, um... yes, I suppose." Lia felt the heat rise in her cheeks as she spoke. What would he think of her?

"Then why don't you show it off more? Pull your dress up and let me see your tits and pussy."

"No. Mistress Ikwo will be coming up soon. You mustn't stay in here."

A grin crossed the man's face. "She's gone out. There's just you and me in the house." He closed the door. "Now, put down the duster and show me how you look."

Lia looked at him for a moment longer, then with a sigh she let her arms fall to her sides, dropping the duster to the floor.

The man gave a low whistle. "You sure are sexy. Lift up the dress."

"No. What do you think I am?"

"Show me. Then I'll leave you alone."

"You'll leave me alone?"

"Sure. Now show me."

Lia paused for a second, then her hands dropped to the hem of her dress. She pulled it up to her waist, her cheeks reddening as the man's eyes fell on her naked pussy.

"Lift it over your tits."

"No, I..."

"Go on. Do it."

Lia bit her lip. She raised the dress, up to her neck, revealing her luscious orbs to the man.

"That's better. Move your legs apart. I wanna get a good look at your cunt."

Lia opened her mouth to protest, then closed it again. Slowly she moved her legs apart, only too aware of the view she was giving to him."

"Shit, you wet down there?"

Lia said nothing, inwardly cursing the recalcitrance of her body as she felt his eyes rove over her nakedness.

"Will you please go now?" she said. "I have to finish my work."

"All in good time." He moved closer to her. "I just wanna feel these pretty tits."

Lia backed away from him.

"C'mon babe. You can't display them to a guy and expect him not to touch them, can you?"

"Please..." Lia's back was against the wall as he closed in on her. As he reached for her breasts she tried to cover them again, but he grabbed her wrists, forcing them behind her, then pinning them together with one large hand while the other closed over the soft orbs.

She tried to struggle free, but the man was too strong for her, his hand roaming freely over her breasts, teasing the nipples to hardness and sending an unwanted thrill through her.

"See, baby, I knew you wanted it," he said, grinning into her face.

"No. I don't."

"Sure you do. Now let's see you proper."

In a single movement he dragged the dress up over Lia's head and down her arms, releasing them briefly as he pulled it off and tossed it aside. He began to knead her breasts again, her erect nipples between finger and thumb.

"You must stop now," she whimpered.

"Not until I've copped a feel down here."

"No!" Lia tried to press her legs together but was again overcome by his strength as he forced her thighs apart, his fingers seeking her vagina. She gasped as she felt them enter her, worming into her sex, rubbing her clitoris and making it swell.

"Shit, it's hot in there," he grinned. "You're ready for it, ain't you?"

He pulled her across the room and pushed her down onto the bed. Then his fingers were sinking into her sex again.

Lia continued to struggle, but the sensations of his intimate probing was becoming too much for her as she writhed under his touch, the juices flowing freely from her vagina as he released her wrists and began groping her bare breasts again.

"That's it. Enjoy."

He moved his fingers back and forth inside her, his thumb rubbing her clitoris in a way that sent spasms of desire through her body. She was not struggling now. Instead she was spreading her legs, her knees bent, her hips thrusting up at his fingers as her passion overwhelmed her, her moans becoming louder with each jab of his fingers.

"Aahh!"

He twisted his fingers inside her vagina, bringing her to new levels of excitement, her backside driving up as she lost herself in lascivious pleasure.

"What on earth?"

The sound of Mistress Ikwo's voice barely registered as Lia writhed in ecstasy. It was not until the man snatched his fingers from her vagina, bringing a groan of disappointment from the girl, that she realized something was wrong. She opened her eyes, and gave a start as she saw the housekeeper staring down at her.

"What is going on?"

The young man jumped to his feet. "It was her. She said she wanted it bad. You can see the way she is. Just look!"

The woman gazed down at Lia, taking in the stiffness of her nipples, the wet trickle escaping her sex and the way her hips were still gyrating as she struggled to bring her body under control.

"Can't you keep your mind off sex for a minute?"

Lia struggled to sit up, closing her legs. "I... I didn't want this."

"What? Just look at you. You're like a bitch on heat."

"But he came in here. He started it."

"Are you surprised, when you flaunt your body like that? Wearing a dress that barely covers your private parts, then taking it off in front of him?"

"I..." Lia's voice trailed away. She dare not admit that her way of dressing was enforced.

The woman turned to the handyman. "Angani, get back to your work. Mister Sagana is not paying you to give pleasure to this dirty little slut."

Sheepishly the man slunk from the room. The housekeeper turned back to Lia, who was still sitting on the bed.

"Get up. It's a good thing I forgot my purse and came back or you would have been fucked by him." She sniffed and cast an eye over Lia's stiff nipples and glistening vagina. "Not that you'd have put up much of a fight."

# Chapter 17

For the next few days Lia was able to settle into the role of Sagana's servant. It was a task to which she was well suited, being a willing and conscientious worker, and she was glad of the fact that, for the most part, it kept her in the background.

Early every morning she would be roused by Mistress Ikwo and sent to perform her ablutions. Then she would pull on a skimpy dress and head down to the kitchen where she would be assigned her tasks. She had been given two of the inadequate dresses by Sagana, and was obliged to daily wash one whilst wearing the other.

Once she was assigned her duties for the day she strived to show herself a good worker, trying her best to please the stern housekeeper. But if the woman felt anything but contempt for her she didn't show it, inspecting her work closely and quick to criticize even the most minor shortcoming.

As for Sagana, Lia assumed he would use her charms like so many before him. But, more like Mbosa, he didn't seem to want her. He was out of the house for much of the day and often long into the evenings. When he arrived home it was Lia's duty to serve him with a glass of whisky, which she would carry to him on a silver tray. The man would take the drink, scarcely casting an eye over her lovely young body, and would then retire to his study to work.

Somehow Lia was unsettled by the reaction. Being kept dressed so provocatively somehow brought out the perverse side of her nature, so that she often found herself turned on by her situation.

It was on the fifth day that Lia was summoned. He had returned home quite late and, as usual, accepted his drink from her before retiring to his study. Lia finished cleaning the kitchen and, when Mistress Ikwo came in, was expecting to be taken upstairs and locked in her room for the night.

The housekeeper told her to get to her feet. "Mister Sagana wants to speak to you."

"To me?"

"Yes. Now get moving."

Lia hurried from the kitchen, trying to arrange her dress to maintain at least a modicum of decency. It was in a state of considerable nervousness that the scantily clad teenager knocked on the door to the study.

"Come in."

She opened the door and stepped inside.

"Close the door."

She did as she was ordered, then moved in front of Sagana's desk. She stood with her arms at her sides, her legs apart, waiting for him to speak.

Sagana had a document open in front of him, which he was studying closely, and it was some minutes before he looked up. When he did so she felt her cheeks flush as he studied her body. At last he spoke.

"So, you've been here for nearly a week now. Are you settling in?"

"Yes Sir, I think so."

"And is Mistress Ikwo treating you properly?"

"She has been very kind to me," replied Lia. It was not strictly true, but the housekeeper, whilst disdainful had not been cruel, and saw to it that she was kept fed.

"And what of your desires?"

"Sir?"

"I understand the plumber was bringing you sexual pleasure."

"He... no, he came into the room where I was working and..."

"I hear you were enjoying it."

"I tried to stop him."

"According to Mistress Ikwo you were naked on the bed, legs spread, moaning with lust."

"He... he was touching me very intimately."

"And you were responding."

Lia said nothing.

"It seems that being naked turns you on."

"I try not to let it."

Sagana gave a half-smile. "I have some guests coming tomorrow night. I expect you to serve them."

"Sir?" Lia felt her heart sink. At least, apart from the handyman she had only been exposed to Sagana and the housekeeper for a few weeks. The thought of strangers intruding was not one she relished.

"They're businessmen, like myself. We'll be having a meeting, after which you'll serve drinks and refreshments."

"Yes, Sir."

"And they might have other requirements of you."

"Other requirements?"

"I expect you to respond to them."

"Yes Sir."

"They'll be arriving at seven o'clock tomorrow. Mistress Ikwo will tell you all you need to know. Right, you can go now."

With her stomach churning at the thought of what she might face the next evening, Lia turned and headed for the door.

# Chapter 18

The sound of the doorbell ringing made Lia start. It was the day after her interview with Sagana, and her sense of anxious anticipation made her jumpy, the knowledge that she was expected to entertain the guests was not something she cared to dwell on.

She listened hard, hearing the housekeeper heading to the front door, then the sound of the door opening. Words were exchanged, then the door closed again, followed by more footsteps making their way into the room next to the one she was in.

She had spent much of the afternoon setting the room up for the meeting. She had extended the dining table and set eight chairs around it. Papers and pencils had been laid out, as well as glasses and jugs of iced water. She made sure the room was spotlessly clean, before being ushered back into the kitchen by Mistress Ikwo.

It was then that she had her first shock. Mistress Ikwo ordered her to go to a cupboard and take out the apron that hung behind the door. It was a short apron with strings to tie behind her neck and around her waist. She turned to the woman.

"I'm supposed to wear this?"

The woman nodded. "Mister Sagana's orders."

"But I..."

"Don't question me, girl. Mister Sagana wants you in the apron. Now put it on."

Lia was surprised. Perhaps Sagana wanted her to look more like a maid. She began at once to put it on, then paused. She thought of Sagana's words when he had taken her in. How she was to show herself to be a slut. She understood, and hesitantly reached for the hem of her skirt and began to lift it.

"What are you doing?"

"I'm going to put on the apron, Mistress."

"But you're taking off your dress."

"Yes, I'm changing."

"But you're removing your dress."

"Did Mister Sagana say I had to keep my dress on?"

"No."

"Then I'll take it off and put the apron on."

The housekeeper opened her mouth to speak again, then closed it, shaking her head.

Lia pulled her skimpy dress over her head and dropped it on the floor. She felt the blood rush to her cheeks as she revealed her body to the housekeeper, standing naked in the kitchen. She picked up the apron, and as the woman watched she set about tying the string behind her neck, then fastening the other one about her waist.

The apron was small, the upper part barely covering her breasts. From the side, she knew her nipples could be seen. The narrow lower part hung barely to the level of her crotch, so that the slightest movement threatened to reveal her pussy. From behind she was completely naked, her shapely bottom on open view.

"You are going to serve the men like that?" asked the housekeeper, clearly aghast.

"I shall serve them in the apron, as my Master has ordered."

"Shameless girl." Mistress Ikwo sniffed. "I can't believe you can be so

83

brazen," she said.

And now the guests were arriving. It had been a relief to Lia that she was not required to open the door to them. Still, she knew she would be required to wait upon them, and the thought of doing so dressed as she was sent a chill through her.

The doorbell rang again, followed by more footsteps and voices. The voices were male, but there was nothing else Lia could tell from them.

Over the next ten minutes the scene was repeated a number of times until all the guests had arrived. Shortly afterwards the housekeeper appeared at the kitchen door.

"They're talking business and will not wish to be disturbed by you," she said curtly. "You will be called for by the bell when they want you."

Lia looked up at the electric buzzer above the kitchen door.

"Yes, Mistress Ikwo. I have to serve them drinks?"

"Of course."

"How will I know what they want?"

"I have taken a list of orders. Prepare them and put them in the fridge. Then wait until you're called."

"Yes, Mistress Ikwo."

Lia took the paper from the woman and spent the next ten minutes mixing cocktails, carefully measuring the amounts and then storing the glasses in the refrigerator.

Then she waited.

The clock hands seemed to turn painfully slowly as she sat in the kitchen, her heart pounding as she anticipated what was to come. She could hear the voices, interspersed with occasional laughter and she wondered what she was to encounter. She wished desperately that they would allow her some more decent clothing, anything to hide her modesty, but she knew she must please Sagana, and that the way she was dressed would do that.

When the bell rang Lia felt her heart sink. She stared at it for a moment, wondering if there was any escape open to her. But deep inside she knew there wasn't. Reluctantly she rose and crossed to the fridge.

With the drinks loaded on the tray she made her way to the meeting room. Outside she put the tray down and knocked.

"Come in."

Lia took a deep breath, then turned the knob and pushed the door open. The lighting in the room was bright. At the table sat Sagana and his eight guests. All were middle-aged men. Every eye was upon her as she stood in the doorway.

"Y-your drinks, Sir."

"Bring them in, girl."

Lia turned and bent down to pick up the tray, only too aware of the sight she was giving the men of her bare backside.

A low whistle sounded from one of them.

"This is your servant?"

84

"Yes."

"And you make her dress like that?"

"No. She chooses to dress like that, don't you girl?"

Lia straightened, holding the tray. "Yes Master."

She made her way into the room and placed the tray on a side table.

"Dry martini?"

"That's mine."

The scantily clad girl carried the drink across to the smiling man, his eyes roving from her breasts to where her pussy was barely covered as she placed the drink before him.

"Gin and tonic?"

"Over here."

One by one Lia served the drinks, her face becoming redder and redder as the men took in her immodest dress. When all were served she picked up the tray and headed for the door, but Sagana pulled her up short.

"No, stay, put the tray down and go and stand there."

He pointed to the middle of the room. Reluctantly Lia made her way across to where he was indicating. She turned to face them, placing her legs apart and dropping her hands to her sides. The men nodded their approval and for a few moments more she was the centre of attention. Then Sagana spoke and a conversation began in Hamite.

For the next hour Lia remained on display. The men talked and laughed, throwing occasional glances in her direction, frequently sending her to refresh their drinks. Lia did her best to remain calm in their company, obeying their orders and fetching the drinks as swiftly as she could.

As she served she noticed the men were becoming freer with their hands. What began as occasional touches as she leant forward in front of them became fondles, hands cupping the cheeks of her backside or stroking the smooth flesh of her thighs. When Lia made no objections they became even more bold, reaching up under the apron and stroking her breasts, laughing as they saw the way her nipples stiffened.

Then, as she was placing a glass in front of a balding man, she felt a hand slide up her inner thigh and a finger trace the slit of her vagina. She made to pull away, but he grasped her leg, his fingers exploring her sex, bringing an unwanted shiver from the near naked girl as she felt a trickle of moisture escape.

She stood, her cheeks glowing as the man continued to finger her. She knew the others could see what was happening, and could see the way her body was responding, her breaths shortening, her hips gyrating slightly.

The man said something to Sagana, who chuckled, then nodded his head. He looked at Lia.

"You like the taste of cock?"

"Sir?"

"You heard me. Do you like to suck cock?"

"I..." Lia felt her throat grow dry. "Yes Master, I love to suck cocks."

"Mister Lugura would like to see how good you are at cock sucking. Show him."

Lia gazed at Sagana for a moment. It was the first demand he had made of her since she'd arrived at his house. She glanced round at the others, watching her expectantly.

"Come on, girl, do as you're told."

"Yes Master."

Lia hesitated a moment longer. Then she dropped to her knees. She got down on all fours, only too aware of the way the apron had dropped from her sex, baring it to the men. She crawled under the table. Under normal circumstances she would have been glad to be away from the men's gaze, but these were not normal circumstances. She turned, so she was facing the man's crotch, glancing nervously between his legs. Then she reached out and began to undo his belt.

She released the button, then pulled down the zipper. Already she could see how his underpants were bulging, as she slid her hand into them and released his cock. It was thick and circumcised and she ran her fingers down its length, squeezing and feeling it swell as she did so. She was aware that some of the men were bent down looking under the table at her. Anxious to please Sagana she moved her legs apart, aware it would give those behind her a perfect view of her pussy.

She leaned forward and opened her lips. She took his cock in her mouth and began to suck, hearing the murmurs from the other men as she did so. It tasted salty as she licked the glans while moving her head up and down, devouring the stiff rod.

"She loves it," said one of the men.

"I told you she's a sex-crazed little slut," replied Sagana. "She came into my bar naked and allowed two strangers to fuck her, one up the ass."

"And you say she belongs to Mbosa?"

"Yes. He plans to come back and take her. Meanwhile, we can enjoy her."

Lia listened to the words as she fellated the man. It sounded odd when Sagana said Mbosa owned her. She felt a slight tremor as she considered what he would do with her. Perhaps she should try to escape before he came back. But where could she go? She had no money and no decent clothes. She was a captive and subject to Sagana's requirements.

Then another of the men spoke. "Hey, Sagana, okay if I get her up on the table? I want to fuck her."

"What about it, girl? You want to be fucked on the table?"

Lia raised her head from the sturdy penis she was sucking. She knew she must respond as Sagana wanted her to.

"Y-yes, Master."

"You want to be fucked?"

"Yes Master, I want to be fucked."

"By anyone in particular?"

"I-I don't mind, Master."

"By all my friends?"

"If they want me, Master."

"Okay guys, looks like she's yours for the evening."

Moments later hands were dragging Lia up, the cock slipping from her mouth again. She was pulled to her feet and turned to face the men.

"You want it, babe?"

"Um, yes, I want it."

"Get rid of the apron."

Hands reached out, undoing the ties, and moments later she was naked in front of the leering men. She stared round at them, her face red as they took in her swelling breasts, her stiff nipples and her smooth crotch, a sheen of wetness visible on her nether lips.

"Very nice."

"Mbosa certainly can pick a slut."

"She looks like she's ready for it."

"Let me have her."

Then hands were grabbing her again, groping her breasts and fingering her sex and ass. Instinctively she tried to resist, but they were determined, their hands exploring her young body, bringing her to a new level of arousal as she gasped and moaned under their hands.

"Get the tart on the table."

Taking hold of her arms and legs they lifted her, laughing at the futility of her struggles. Roughly they pushed her onto the table on her back.

Her legs were dragged apart and she was pulled forward so her open sex was at the table edge. Fingers probed her again, bringing more involuntary gasps of pleasure from her as they teased her clitoris and sank deep into her. The man she had been sucking moved round to stand by her head, grabbing her hair and rolling her head to face his rampant erection. Lia opened her mouth and took it back inside, amid the jeers of the watching men.

No sooner was she sucking the erection in her mouth, than she gave a muffled gasp as another stiff cock was pressed against her open sex. She gave a low moan as it penetrated her, the wetness of her vagina allowing it to slide in easily.

"Give it to her, Lane."

"Bitch is dying for it."

"Fuck the little whore."

The man began to fuck her hard, slamming his hips against hers as his penis thrust deep into her vagina, each thrust shaking her body and bringing muffled cries from the wanton beauty as her own arousal began to increase.

As she fucked and sucked other hands descended on her, grabbing hold of her breasts, pinching the nipples and slapping the soft flesh. And Lia was submitting to their desires, allowing them to use her as they wished.

"Shit, the babe's loving it," gasped the man whose cock was embedded in her vagina.

Lia knew he could feel the way her sex walls were pulsating about his thick penis, and that they could see her arousal as she avidly sucked the cock in her mouth, her hands caressing the weighty balls hanging beneath.

"Oh yeah!"

The man gave a gasp of pleasure and her mouth filled with hot spunk as he spurted into her. She gulped down his semen, swallowing as more and more pumped into her throat, some of it leaking from the corners of her mouth and dribbling onto the table, much to the amusement of those watching.

"Hey babe, I got more of that for you."

"She's a real spunk bucket."

The bald man withdrew and another eager cock was plunged between her lips, her body jerking back and forth as the other man fucked her hard.

Lia could sense his arousal increasing, and with that came an increase in her own excitement, her body pressing back against his, her breath coming in gasps as she felt him stiffen even more. As he came she came too, writhing with unwanted pleasure as she felt spunk pumping into her vagina, her hips thrusting upward, her ass slapping down on the table as she responded to the extraordinary orgasm.

He pulled his cock from her, a dribble of sperm leaking onto her thigh as he did. Lia relaxed, but only for a moment before she found herself dragged over onto her stomach, her head pulled up so she could fellate another one. She gave a gasp as another penis pressed against her anus, hands pulling the cheeks of her backside apart as he thrust, bringing a cry from her as he forced his cock into her asshole.

For the next hour Lia's mind was a blur as the men used her body at will. She lost count of the number of times her mouth, vagina and rectum were filled with spunk, her lovely young body maneuvered into every possible position to satisfy the group. She was overwhelmed by the experience, orgasm after orgasm shaking her form as she screamed and moaned her desire, every orgasm accompanied by the goading of the men as they saw how she reacted to their treatment, writhing about on the table.

At last they were done, the last ones zipping up their pants. Lia lay exhausted on the table, her legs spread, her sperm-spattered breasts rising and falling as she regained her breath. The men were leaving, some not even bothering to glance back at the girl.

Only Sagana remained, and Lia realized he had not touched her. He rose to his feet, gazing down at the ravaged youngster, an expression of distaste on his face.

"Get yourself cleaned up," was all he said, and walked out the room.

# Chapter 19

The weeks passed and Lia continued her existence as a servant and sex toy. After a while she was surprised to note that despite the depravity of her situation, she almost found herself in a routine under Sagana's control.

Her daily duties of cleaning and polishing would be supervised closely by the housekeeper as the young beauty strived to please the stern woman. Then at least once a week she would be called into the presence of Sagana's colleagues, where she would be used for their pleasure. After the first occurrence she would attend them naked, much to the displeasure of the housekeeper. Once she had served the drinks she'd have to perform, sucking and fucking, sometimes with a dozen men, often for hours on end.

She began to know the men, and their preferences, offering them her mouth, vagina or anus as they called her to them. There were often newcomers as well, all with perverse desires she was obliged to satisfy. Some would want to spank her backside or breasts. Others would make her masturbate with various objects. And during these episodes Sagana would always remain aloof, watching but not touching.

But suddenly things changed. It began with a chance encounter She had been cleaning the small toilet next to the kitchen. She was busily scrubbing the sink when she heard Sagana enter the kitchen. The sound of another man's voice sent a shiver through her; any male visitor often meant she would be summoned for him to enjoy.

The men were clearly unaware that she was so close, able to hear as they talked. She had not intended to eavesdrop, but the words she heard made her freeze and listen intently.

"So Mbosa's coming back for her tomorrow?"

"That's what he says. He reckons the heat's off him now, so he can afford to come and get her."

"Well it's a shame. She's a real find. So what's Mbosa gonna do with her?"

"Take her back to Hamita and sell her."

"White slave like that should fetch a good price."

"I don't think he's bothered about the money. He just wants to let a white girl know what it's like to be considered inferior."

"Well, she'll certainly see that."

"Right, let's go to the office. I want to discuss some of those proposals you sent me yesterday."

The men's voices faded as they made their way out of the kitchen. Lia stood frozen to the spot, turning their words over in her mind. Tomorrow Mbosa was coming to claim her as his. To take her to his country and sell her. The words "white slave" rang in her brain as she considered her fate. Being Sagana's housemaid and his friends' sexual plaything was bad, but the thought of what Mbosa had planned for her sounded much worse.

But what could she do? She was a virtual prisoner in the house. When Mistress Ikwo was not there the doors were always locked, and at night she was kept in a virtual cell. There seemed to be no escape.

A knocking sound from upstairs made her pause in her thoughts. The handyman, Angani, was working on the upstairs bathroom. Lia thought of the time he had tried to seduce her. It was clear that Mistress Ikwo had a firm word with him, as he never again attempted to touch her. Still, she had been aware of his hungry looks when she encountered him around the house, and she knew he wanted her. Slowly the possibility of a plan began to form in her mind.

She glanced at the clock. Ikwo had gone out on her errands about half an hour earlier, which gave her about another fifteen minutes before her return. Did she dare approach the handyman? She hesitated a moment longer, then the words "white slave" came back to her. Taking a deep breath she crept for the kitchen and made her way on tiptoe to the stairs.

When she reached the upstairs bathroom she hesitated once more, stepping back to examine herself in the full length mirror. As usual she was wearing the skimpy dress, her breasts barely covered by the thin cloth, the short skirt threatening at any moment to expose her pussy. A shudder ran through her as she considered how slutty she looked. She glanced at the door of the bathroom. For a moment her confidence escaped her and she turned back towards the stairs, but she remembered Sagana's words. Taking a deep breath she moved across to the bathroom and opened the door.

The young Hamite was on his knees by the basin, a wrench in his hand. As she entered he turned, his eyes taking in her beautiful body.

"Sorry, babe, can't use this bathroom. I'm working."

"I-I didn't want to use the bathroom."

"Then what you doing in here?"

"I came to speak to you, Mister Angani."

He put down his tool and rose to his feet. Lia had forgotten how tall he was, and as he approached she felt a shiver run through her.

"What you wanna talk about?"

She took a deep breath. "About you and me."

"Me and you? What you getting at?"

"Well, that time when you..." her voice trailed away as she felt the heat in her cheeks increase.

"You want some more?"

"I... yes, I want some more."

Angani reached out, stroking her cheek. Lia wanted to back away, but knew she mustn't.

"You wanna take that dress off?"

"No, there isn't time. Mistress Ikwo will be back soon."

"What then?"

"Take me away from here."

"Take you away?"

90

"Yes. Please. Come for me tonight."

"Why don't you get away yourself?"

"I'm can't. My room's locked at night."

"So how can I get you out?"

Lia indicated his tools. "You could do it."

His hand slid down from her cheek, her slender neck, then lower, slipping inside her dress and cupping her firm breast.

"You want me?"

Lia didn't falter. "Yes, I want you."

"Show me your room."

She led the Hamite up the stairs, down the corridor to her room. The bars on the window were hinged at one side, held closed by a padlock. Angani studied it, then nodded.

"I can cut through that so no one would notice."

"Will you?"

He pulled her close, his lips closing over hers. His hand slipped under her dress and she felt his fingers trace her sex lips, lingering on her clitoris, bringing a surge of arousal to the girl as his tongue probed hers. Then he was pushing her away again.

"You gonna be able to climb down?"

"Yes, I can use my sheets."

"Ten o'clock then."

"Ten o'clock." Lia went to the door, needing to get back downstairs. "And please bring something for me to wear."

"That dress is fine."

"I'm not allowed it at night."

She saw a faint grin cross his features.

"Okay," he said. "Ten o'clock."

He turned his attention to the padlock.

# Chapter 20

Lia sat at the window of her room, gazing out into the darkness. She had no means of reading the time, but she knew it must be close to ten o'clock and her heart was beating fast as she contemplated what she was doing.

She knew it was dangerous. She was already on the run from the Bikers, and to make Hamite enemies was not something she wanted. But she feared Mbosa and his intentions, and the thought of putting herself back under his power was not something she wished to contemplate.

A sound reached her ears, and she froze. Below, a twig broke underfoot. There was someone out there. She glanced down at herself. She was naked, having been forced by Mistress Ikwo to wash her dress and hang it in the bathroom before being locked in her room, as happened every night. Normally it didn't bother her that she was obliged to sleep naked, but tonight was different and she wished she had something to cover her. She wasn't even able to wrap a sheet about her body, since both her sheets were tied together in a makeshift escape rope.

She squinted out of the window, and caught sight of movement. Moments later Angani stepped into the dim light from the moon. He was looking up at her window and beckoning to her.

Her heart pounding, Lia removed the doctored padlock and pushed the bars open, biting her lip anxiously as she heard the squeaking hinges. She checked the sheet was securely fastened to the radiator and climbed onto the window sill.

She wondered at the sight she must make, naked in the moonlight as she maneuvered herself over the sill and began lowering herself to the ground. The sheets were not long enough, and she found herself hanging about six feet above the lawn, so taking a deep breath she let go and dropped, rolling over as she landed. She found herself gazing up into the face of Angani, who was standing over her.

He reached down and pulled her to her feet, then he was dragging her behind him, heading into the woods.

"Where are we going?" she whispered.

"Just keep quiet," he responded.

For the next few minutes Lia found herself almost running through the dense forest behind him, often nearly falling over as she struggled to keep up with him. The house disappeared behind them as they made their way swiftly along narrow tracks. It was clear he knew the woods well, as to Lia it was a maze of featureless trees and bushes.

At last she caught sight of a vehicle parked in the trees. It was an old car, and even in the moonlight she could discern the rust and faded paintwork, but it was with some relief that she realized they had accomplished the first part of her plan.

Angani turned to face her, and Lia was reminded of her lack of clothing as he cast his eyes over her body, taking in her panting breasts, then letting his eyes drop to her naked mound.

"Do you have some clothes for me?" she asked nervously.

"Why bother?" he replied. "You look pretty good to me as you are."

"I need clothes."

He moved closer to her. "Not right now," he said.

Lia knew what he wanted. He intended to enjoy her body here and now. In her heart she'd known that might be the price of him rescuing her, but had tried not to think about it. He reached out and ran a hand over the soft flesh of her breasts. Lia fought down the urge to back away, staring up into his face as he teased her nipples into hard buds, kneading the swelling orbs and bringing shivers of excitement to the teenager.

"You have a very sexy body," he said.

Lia didn't reply, trying hard not to respond to his caresses.

"Who fucked you last?" he asked.

Lia dropped her eyes. "I don't know."

"You don't know?"

"I mean, I didn't know his name."

He gave a small grin, his hand continuing to caress her breast. "You fuck with men you don't know?"

"It was Mister Sagana who wanted me to do it. I had to obey."

He moved his hand down, across the soft flatness of her belly, down to her pubic mound, his fingers seeking her slit. Lia pressed her legs together.

"Please..."

"You don't like being touched here?"

"Y-you mustn't. I need some clothes."

"All in good time." He reached a hand about her neck, pulling her face close to his, his other hand continuing to trace her sex lips. "Look at me."

He was tall, towering over the naked girl, so she had to look up at him.

"You asked for my help, and I gave it to you. Now it's your turn. Open your legs."

For a moment Lia hesitated. Then with a sigh she moved her feet apart.

"That's better." He pressed a finger against the entrance to her vagina, bringing a gasp from the young beauty as it penetrated her. He continued to gaze down into her eyes as his fingers explored her, and the expression on his face told her that he could feel the way the muscles of her love tunnel were contracting about them, as well as the wetness already seeping out.

He pressed her back against the hood of the old car, and Lia shivered as she felt the cold metal against her bare backside. He continued to press until she was laying back on the hood.

"Spread your legs wider."

Lia obeyed, exposing the pinkness of her sex to his hungry eyes. She groaned as he pressed his fingers still deeper, causing her to involuntarily push her hips up against his hand.

He leaned forward and began to caress her breasts once more, bringing new spasms of excitement to the girl, her breath shortening as he explored her. Despite her predicament she was rapidly reaching the stage where her body was beyond control, her naked form writhing beneath his touch.

"You wanna taste some black cock?" His face was right above hers, looking down into her eyes as his hands explored her. "Sure you do. C'mon."

He took hold of her wrist, guiding her hand down to the bulge at the front of his jeans. Passion shook her as she felt his hardness, and almost automatically she undid the button and lowered the zipper. She slipped her hand inside. He was wearing briefs, the thin material barely able to contain his swollen cock. There was a sense of urgency as she pulled the material down, allowing his huge penis to spring out.

He was still fingering her as she wrapped her hand around it. She was in his power now, her lascivious nature taking control as she squeezed his erection and began masturbating him. Then his face was close to hers again.

"C'mon, slut, suck me."

He removed his fingers, bringing a sigh from her. Then he pulled her up off the hood, her eyes fixed on his erection as she dropped to her knees, her fingers still wrapped about its stem. She leant forward, opened her lips and took it into her mouth.

It smelt and tasted of male arousal and she began to suck greedily, her tongue licking his glans. Now it was his turn to groan as she fellated him with vigour, her head moving back and forth, her breasts shaking deliciously as she sucked, a trail of moisture running down her thigh from her pulsating sex.

He grabbed her hair and thrust his hips against her face, fucking it hard. Lia found herself gasping for breath, her mouth filled with cock as he rammed it into her. Still she sucked, her fingers caressing his balls, her hair swaying as he rammed his thick weapon into her. He came with a grunt, his cock spurting hot semen into her mouth. Lia swallowed enthusiastically, still sucking as she drank his seed.

At last he was slowing, his ejaculation dwindling to a dribble. His penis slipped from her mouth as she knelt before him, gazing up into his face.

"Shit, you're some cocksucker," he murmured.

# Chapter 21

"But where are we going?"

"You'll see."

"Will there be people?"

"That worry you?"

"I... I can't meet people like this."

"Sure you can. You know you'll enjoy it."

Lia bit her lip and glanced down at what she was wearing, a shiver running through her. "Did you bring me clothes, like you promised?"

"I said I would, didn't I?"

Lia was anxious to cover herself. She watched expectantly as Angani opened a door of the car and pulled something out. He tossed it to her. She looked down at the small bundle of cloth with increasing anxiety. It was a soft netting, somewhat like a string vest, but flimsier.

"Is this it?"

"Put it on."

Lia held the garment out in front of her, taking in its form. The lower part was a skirt; a short wraparound skirt, with black tapes to hold it together.

"Put it on, I said."

She glanced at Angani. He was watching her, stern-faced. Gingerly she wrapped the skirt about herself, tying the tapes in a bow at her hip, leaving a slit at the side that clearly revealed her lack of panties. The garment was made of a soft, stretchable material that clung to her legs. It hugged her hips, precisely following the curves of her body.

The rest of the garment consisted of two strips of cloth about three inches wide attached to the waist of the skirt by a metal ring. She pulled it up and behind her neck, where she tied it with two more tapes, tucking the bow under her hair. Then she arranged the cloth so that it covered her breasts, her stiff nipples protruding through the mesh.

Lia stood, her hands at her sides as the man ran his eyes over her. The material clung to her like a second skin, and she knew her pussy lips were just exposed. The upper part left her breasts barely covered too, her nipples on display.

"Couldn't I have some underwear?" she asked.

Angani shook his head. "You look fine like that," he said. "Now get in the car."

He drove out of the wood onto an open road. Lia gazed out of the window as they traveled. They were coming into a more populated area, and as she looked at the houses passing she felt her anxiety growing. She had wanted to escape from Mbosa, but what was she letting herself in for? The man beside her clearly had little sympathy for her situation, and had shown interest only in her ability to turn him on. The skimpy clothing confirmed to her that, like so many men, he saw her as little more than a sex object. Now he was clearly driving with a purpose, but to where?

As they traveled further into the town the buildings became bigger and less scruffy. Lia saw people on the streets, increasing her nervousness as she considered how she was dressed. Most of the people she saw were Hamites, but increasingly she was seeing other people. Then Angani swung the wheel to the left and pulled up in a small parking lot outside a large building.

Lia glanced at him anxiously. "Where are we?"

"A fun place. Get out."

She glanced down at herself. "Couldn't I stay here?"

"What the hell for? Don't you want some fun?"

"I... I just want..."

"Get out, baby. C'mon."

Reluctantly Lia reached for her door handle. As she stepped from the car she glanced about. To her relief there was nobody in sight, but still her heart was beating hard as she watched Angani lock the car, and then beckon her to join him. He linked his arm through hers and led her towards the building.

Like so many others it had a rundown look, tatty and intimidating. At the front were steps that led down, like some kind of pedestrian subway, lit by a flickering fluorescent light. As they began to descend Lia saw a faded sign. It was an arrow pointing downwards with *Cisco's* written across it.

Music reached her ears. It was clearly some kind of club and she tried to draw back, but Angani held firmly to her arm, pulling her along.

"What is this place?" she asked.

"Somewhere people have fun," he replied.

"But, this dress..."

"Looks good on you. Come on."

At the bottom of the steps was a red door with *Cisco's* over the top. Outside stood a brute of a man, in a suit and dark glasses.

"Hey, Angani," he said.

"Hey, Sabato."

The two men high-fived one another.

"Who's the babe?"

"Just this chick who fancies me. Say hi to Sabato, babe."

"H-hello," Lia stammered.

The man ran his eyes over her. "She always dress like that?"

"Sure. She likes the attention."

The man shook his head. "She's sure gonna get some in there."

"That's what she likes. C'mon, baby."

Sabato pulled the door open, the music became much louder, and Angani pushed her into the club.

# Chapter 22

Lia looked about. They were on a balcony from which a staircase ran down into the large room. Below was a dancefloor where many people were gyrating with enthusiasm. Beyond the dancefloor was a long bar, at which more people were clustered. Many of them spilled over into an area of tables and chairs.

The general lighting was dim, but bright lights swung back and forth across the dancers as the music throbbed out a beat. The air was warm and heavy with cigarette smoke. There were other smoke scents as well, which Lia suspected were not legal.

She noticed with some surprise that there was a mixture of races, almost as many white people as Hamites. In the segregated societies to which she was accustomed this was somewhat unusual, but she had heard of such places. As Angani led her down the steps she observed that they were far from being the only mixed race couple in the club.

At first, to her relief, few people were looking in her direction. Most of the women, she noticed, were dressed in short skirts and at first glance she would appear to be little different, although even if it hadn't been totally see-through, her dress would have been rather outrageous. But she noticed more heads turning in her direction, some clubbers pointing as they saw her.

Angani led her to the bar. Lia wanted to hold back as the lights were brighter there, but he pulled her along. More eyes were turning in her direction, taking in the swell of her breasts, her nipples clearly visible as they jutted through the thin black netting.

Angani flagged down a barman. "Two beers."

"Sure." The barman placed two bottles down on the bar. Angani took one and thrust the other into Lia's hand. Then he turned and looked about.

"Hey, Angani, who's the babe?"

It was a young white man. His arm was around an attractive blonde.

"Hi Steve, Anya. How you doing?"

"This your girl?"

"She's with me right now. What do you think?"

Lia eyed the couple. The man was in his early twenties, with cropped hair, dressed in light slacks and a polo shirt. His girlfriend was of a similar age, wearing a low top and a miniskirt, her face heavily made-up. She was observing Lia with some amusement.

"Nice dress," she said.

Angani grinned. "She likes it," he said. "Thinks it makes her look sexy."

Steve let his eyes run over Lia's body. "Yeah, I guess it does. Hey Anya, how come you don't wear stuff like that?"

"Because I'm not a slut."

The men laughed, and Lia felt the blood rising in her cheeks.

"So babe, fancy a dance?" Angani placed an arm about her shoulders, his hand slipping under the thin dress and openly caressing her breast, making Anya smile condescendingly at Lia.

"I..." Lia faltered.

"Sure you do. You wanna show off the dress, don't you? C'mon."

Still openly fondling her he led her onto the dancefloor. When he removed his hand her breast was left completely exposed and she quickly covered it again, although the flimsy netting offered her no modesty at all. He dropped into the beat of the music and Lia began to dance too, her hips gyrating as she tried to lose herself and block from her mind the sight she made. She was only too aware that the eyes of most of the men were upon her as she danced, as well as of the whistles and calls of those around her.

They danced for a few numbers, then Angani led her back to the bar, this time with his hand under her skirt squeezing her bare buttock. When they re-joined Steve and Anya the pair were with a larger crowd, mainly young men, and Lia felt her embarrassment increase as she stood before them.

"Hey Angani, nice chick."

"Bet she's a good fuck."

"Need any help with keeping her satisfied?"

"Looks like she needs it. Look at those nipples!"

Lia glanced down. It was true, her nipples were protruding through the gauze of her dress, betraying the unwelcome excitement she felt at being so exposed.

"Can I dance with her, Angani?"

Lia glanced up in alarm. The man was white, about twenty-five years old, wearing a white T-shirt and jeans. He moved close, a grin on his face.

"Sure, Joey. She's not mine. Just came with me."

The man took Lia's arm. "C'mon babe."

Lia resisted for a second, then allowed herself to be led back to the dancefloor. The man pulled her to him, pressing his body against hers as he dropped into the beat of the music. Lia felt his hand drop to her backside, caressing the firm globes as he held her close. Joey was taller than her and she found her face pressed against his chest as he held her. Despite her embarrassment she found herself swaying with him to the rhythm of the music.

"You look fucking sexy in that dress," he said.

"Th-thank you."

"You like showing off your tits and cunt like that?"

"I... Angani gave me the dress."

"You didn't have to take it."

"I needed something to wear."

"You must have been walking about naked."

Lia didn't answer, causing the man to stare down at her.

"You were naked?"

"Yes."

The man gave a low whistle. "I'd like to have seen that. I bet it turned you on." He squeezed her closer, his hands roving over her back. "Is this turning you on?"

"No, I..."

"It sure seems to be. Is it making your cunt wet?"

She said nothing.

"Let's check it out."

"No, please..."

He ignored her protest, a hand pushing up her skirt, then closing over the lips of her sex.

Lia was unable to suppress a cry as she felt his fingers enter her vagina, sliding inside her while his thumb pressed her swollen clitoris.

"Shit, you're really wet. You some kind of exhibitionist?"

Lia bit her lip. It was true that being exposed as she was had once again aroused a perverse desire within her. Despite her shame at showing herself so publicly there was an excitement as well as she felt the eyes of people on her body.

She let out a groan as he pressed his fingers deeper, sending a new surge of lust through her.

"Yeah, you wanna show yourself off, don't you?"

"No I..."

He moved his left hand up to her neck, taking hold of the tape that held the top part of her dress and pulling undone. Lia gave a cry of distress as she felt the material pulled away, exposing her breasts. Then he was tugging at the tape at her waist.

"Please don't," she begged.

"Come on, babe, you know you want to show everything."

"But all these people..."

"They wanna see it too."

Lia gave a gasp of dismay as she felt the skirt fall from her. He pulled the dress from her and tossed it aside. Lia was so shocked by the move that for a moment she just stood, frozen as she felt all eyes in the room upon her.

A cheer went up, ringing in her ears as she stood on the dancefloor completely naked. Then he was holding her close once more while his fingers continued to explore her sex.

Lia's mind was a blur of confusion as she found herself naked in the middle of the busy club. More than anything she wanted to run and hide as she heard laughter, whistles and catcalls. She buried her face in the man's chest, not wishing to catch the eyes of the other clubbers in her shameful state.

"There," he said, "that's how you like to be, isn't it?"

He pressed his fingers deeper into her vagina, his thumb continuing to toy with her love bud. Lia could feel the wetness leaking out onto his hand. As happened so often her body was not obeying her mind as pulses of excitement swept through her. She wondered at the way her body responded. She was being held by a man she didn't know while his fingers explored her intimately. Yet again she felt her resistance slipping away as her traitorous body responded.

"Shit, you really are enjoying this, aren't you?"

Lia struggled to free herself, but her ignominy was overcome by sexual desire as he continued to finger her.

"Let's show the folks how excited you are," he said, turning her round. She fought him for a moment, then surrendered, allowing him to turn her until she was facing the watching clubbers, giving them an unrestricted view of her naked body.

He relaxed his grip on her, clearly sensing she was surrendering to her perverse desires. "Little exhibitionist," he murmured in her ear, his fingers probing her sex again as his other hand moved up from her waist and began to caress her jutting breasts. She found herself thrusting her hips against his hand, her legs spread, her knees bent, gasping with desire.

"Shit, look at that."

"Bitch is on heat."

"Squeeze those tits, Joey."

"Yeah, give her what she wants."

The remarks stung Lia, yet in a strange way they increased her arousal. Being naked and being masturbated in front of a crowd of strangers was bringing a fresh layer of excitement to her, her gasps increasing as her hips gyrated.

Then suddenly he stopped, his hands leaving her breasts and sex, dragging a moan of anguish from her. He continued to hold her, facing those watching, his hands at her waist as she tried to regain control.

"Okay babe?" he murmured in her ear. "You must like dancing with me. For a moment there I thought you were going to come."

He pushed her back to where Angani was standing, as the sneers and mocking laughter about her continued.

# Chapter 23

Lia looked about, searching for the dress. It gave her only the minimum of modesty, but at least it was something.

"Enjoy your dance?" said Angani. "You sure looked like you did."

"M-my dress."

"Took it off, I see. You sure enjoy being naked, don't you?"

"It was him. He took it off me."

"And boy did that turn you on. I thought you was going to come right there."

"Too right," said Joey. "Boy, is her pussy wet."

He moved close behind her again, fingers cupping her breast while others slipped again into the heat and wetness of her sex. Lia found herself leaning back against him, spreading her legs, her knees buckled as she pressed her hips down with an abandoned moan. She knew the sight she must make, naked and shameless before these people, her head thrown back as she was publicly masturbated.

"Bitch needs it bad," he said.

"Yeah," put in Anya. She ran a hand over Lia's bare breast, toying with the protruding teat and bringing a fresh gasp from the naked girl.

Two young men stepped forward. Lia tried to draw back, but Joey remained behind her blocking her way. Then they were touching her, rough hands squeezing her breasts.

"Nice tits."

"And she sure likes having them touched."

Lia bit her lip, trying not to respond. Then she felt another hand close on her bum, caressing the soft flesh. She tried to break away, but more hands were reaching for her, the crowd pressing in as they saw how available she was. She began to struggle, but Joey's strong hands closed about her arms, holding her where she was.

More hands were crawling over her body, grasping her naked flesh, bringing fresh gasps from her as again she felt control slipping from her. She stopped struggling, her breath coming in short gasps, her sex weeping juices as her hips thrust down on the fingers penetrating her. More men were pushing to get a feel of her, as well as some of the women, and she was abandoning herself to them, her body alive with desire.

"Enough!"

The voice was loud, full of authority. For a moment the hands continued to grope Lia's naked flesh.

"Enough, I said!"

The hands began to fade away, men and women moving back. Lia stood alone in a circle of onlookers, staggering to stay upright, her body alive with sexual desire. The crowd stood aside, and she saw the man they who had ordered them to stop.

It was Mbosa. Lia felt a shiver of fear run through her as she found herself facing the man. She had almost forgotten the coldness of his eyes, but she felt it now as he ran them over her naked body, his face grim.

"Don't you ever wear clothes?"

"I... I had a dress but..."

"Who brought you here?"

Lia looked about, but could see no sign of Angani. She guessed he had spotted Mbosa and made himself scarce. It was clear the man was feared and respected, and not just by Hamites. Everyone looked rattled by Mbosa's appearance.

"Well, who was it? His name."

"I don't know," she lied. Despite the way Angani had treated her she was reluctant to name him.

"You know," said Mbosa. "But it isn't important, because I know too. I'll be talking to him later."

Lia said nothing.

"Now you are back in my possession, do you understand me?"

She hung her head. "Yes."

"You're coming with me now."


Lia stepped from the shower and reached for a towel. She had been under the water for more than ten minutes, washing and relaxing in the warmth of it.

The drive from the club had been a long one. Lia had no idea how long as she fell into a deep sleep, despite the discomfort of the trunk. She awoke to find herself staring up at daylight as Mbosa raised the lid, then she was ordered out.

She had found herself in front of a house in a scruffy street. Fortunately there was nobody around, and when Mbosa opened the front door she hurried inside, anxious to hide her nakedness. He sent her straight upstairs to the bathroom, ordering her to clean herself up, then report to him downstairs. She had not needed to be told twice. Once inside she stepped into the shower, turning on the water and letting it soothe her body.

As she dried herself she began to wonder at her predicament. Where was she? Why had she been brought here? What did Mbosa intend to do with her?

She hung the towel back on the rail and glanced about. There were no clothes of any kind in the room. She considered wrapping the towel about her, but guessed that to do so would not please Mbosa.

"Girl! Get down here!"

There was no mistaking the impatience in Mbosa's voice. Taking a hasty look at her nakedness in the mirror, she turned and opened the bathroom door.

As she headed for the stairs a flash of light caught Lia's eye and she glanced out of the landing window, apprehension gripping her. The light was the reflection of the sun off water, and as she gazed out she saw they were on the coast. She saw docks, with massive ships being unloaded by cranes. Lia had never seen the sea before, but she knew that dockland towns and cities were rough, lawless places. Even the Bikers gave them a wide berth, having tried and failed to gain control in many. Most of the inhabitants were Hamites, dockworkers and sailors, and the Bikers allowed them their way, restricting their control to taking taxes from the truck drivers who streamed in and out of such places. As she gazed out at the ships Lia wondered what was to become of her.

She descended the stairs. Opposite the door through which she had entered the building was another. It was closed, but she could hear voices behind it. She took a deep breath, then tapped on the door.

"Get in here!"

Lia pushed the door open and stepped inside. Mbosa was sitting in an easy-chair facing the door. On either side of him sat two black men. Both were about mid-twenties, wearing suits and ties. Lia shivered slightly as she felt their gaze on her naked body. She wanted to cover herself, but instead she walked across to stand in front of the three.

"This is the girl," said Mbosa.

"Hmm, not bad," said one of the men. "She looks an innocent little thing."

"May look innocent, but she fucks like a bunny." Mbosa looked keen to conclude whatever their business was. "So, you'll take her?"

One of the men rose to his feet and moved closer to her, his eyes roving over her naked flesh. Lia stood still as he walked around her, inspecting her body. He was tall, over six feet, and he radiated a similar confidence to that shown by Mbosa, making her feel very nervous.

He stopped, facing her, then reached out and took her breast in his hand, making her shiver slightly as he toyed with it. Lia was aware of the nipple puckering instantly, and of the message this would send to him.

"Open your legs."

It was an order. Lia widened her stance at once.

The man reached down, bringing a small gasp from the girl as his fingers sought her clitoris. He toyed with it, then slipped a finger into her vagina. Lia tried her best to stay motionless, not to react, but she knew he would feel the convulsions in her sex as he fingered her, the walls pulsing about his probing digit.

He withdrew his finger and held it up. It was shiny and wet with her juices.

"Lick it."

Lia leant forward and took his finger into her mouth, sucking her love juices from it. When she had finished the man turned to his companion.

"She'll do," he said.

102

# Chapter 24

Lia opened her eyes and blinked up at a bare ceiling. There was a dull ache in her head, and her eyelids felt heavy as she slowly regained consciousness. She tried to remember where she was. She recalled that the three men had made her lie down on the floor of the room. At the time she thought they were going to fuck her. She remembered seeing Mbosa's face as he loomed over her, then a strange-smelling cloth was clamped over her mouth and nose.

Then nothing.

She must have been drugged. But why? And how long had she been unconscious? She tried to sit up, but couldn't, and realized she was in bondage.

She raised her head. She was lying on a narrow bed, with a thin mattress and no other bedding. She was completely naked. At her wrists and ankles were strong leather bonds. As she pulled at them she saw they were attached by metal chains to the corners of the bed. She was spread-eagled and helpless, totally vulnerable.

She looked around. She was in a small room, lit by a fluorescent strip lamp on the ceiling. On one wall was a very solid looking door, made of metal, on another a smaller door which was open, revealing a bathroom. Apart from the bed, the only other furnishing was a metal table and chair. The walls were painted an off-white. There were pipes running across just below the ceiling, and on one wall was a circular metal object that was bolted down. Her ears were filled with a dull mechanical sound, like the roar of air conditioning.

But most alarming of all, the room was moving. She was on a ship! The circular object on the wall was covering a porthole. The movement was the rolling of the vessel as it moved through the water.

She was at sea!

Dread filled her. Hadn't Mbosa said he would take her back to his country? Hadn't she been told she would be sold, enslaved by some wealthy Hamite? She tugged at the bonds, but she knew she was helpless, and it was too late. She was truly Mbosa's now, and there was nothing she could do about it.

She lay, gazing up at the deck head as time passed. Occasionally she would hear the sound of a voice, or footsteps outside, but otherwise she was alone.

Eventually she heard footsteps stop at the door, and the sound of a key in the lock. Lia tensed. The door opened and a man stepped into the cabin. Lia gazed at him in apprehension. He was a black man of about fifty, dressed in a rather shabby blue uniform, his cuffs decorated with gold stripes. He wore a cap with a white brim and a faded badge. He turned and locked the door again, slipping the key into his pocket. He moved across to where the beautiful girl lay, his eyes wandering over her naked flesh. Lia closed her eyes, unable to meet his gaze.

"So, this is Mbosa's merchandise," he said, his voice deep in the small cabin.

Lia heard the scrape of the chair being brought up to the side of the bed, then a sigh as the man sat down.

"Look at me."

She kept her eyes shut. Then gave a cry of surprise and pain as a hand swatted across her breast.

"Look at me!"

Her cheeks glowing, the naked girl opened her eyes, meeting the man's stern gaze.

"You know where you are?"

"On... on a ship, Sir?"

"That's right. On my ship."

"Yours?"

"I am Captain Ngoru. You correctly referred to me as Sir. That is how you will address me."

"Y-yes, Sir."

"Do you know where you are going?"

"To Hamita Sir?"

"Yes. To Hamita. My country. Do you know why you are going there?"

"I... I think I am to be sold, Sir."

"Hmm. Yes. And I think you'll make a good price."

Lia gave a start as she felt the Captain's hand touch her. His palm was rough as he ran it over her belly, yet still she felt an unwelcome shiver of stimulation as he touched her naked flesh, a sensation perversely increased by her nudity and bondage.

"You allow men to use you?"

"S-Sir?"

"This body. You surrender it to men?"

"I... I do as I am told, Sir."

The man moved his hand up, placing it over her breast, his eyes fixed on hers as he squeezed the tender flesh.

"And you once belonged to the Bikers?"

"Yes Sir."

He rose to his feet, his eyes still roving over her naked flesh.

"You will be on my ship for a few more days," he said. "During that time I will be your master. Do you understand?"

Lia felt the blood rise in her cheeks again. It was clear to her what the man was saying. She gave a little nod.

"Good. Now you have a choice. If you pledge to obey me, I will allow you some freedom. I will allow you to eat with me, and to leave this cabin under guard. If you betray my trust you will eat naked with the crew. Understand?"

Lia understood. She was to obey him and do everything he told her to do, or she was to be thrown to his crew. He already had full control over her, and he was also demanding her obedience. She knew she had no option.

"You are my master," she said quietly.

The man nodded. "Good."

104

He leant over her and fiddled with the lock that held her wrist, and her arm was free. He did the same with her other arm, and her legs.

When the bonds were undone Lia felt an urge to cover her naked body and hide it from his gaze. But she knew that would displease him, so she remained as she was, lying on her back, her legs parted.

"Good," he said, running a hand down between her legs and toying briefly with her exposed clitoris. "I will see you in my cabin in an hour."

The hour passed slowly. She was grateful for the opportunity to freshen up beneath the tepid shower, using soap and shampoo she found by the small metal sink.

There was a threadbare towel hanging beside the shower and she used it to dry herself off. She stepped back into the cabin and saw a small door she hadn't noticed before. She pulled it open, and gave a little squeal of delight as she saw a dress hanging inside. It was small, made of thin cheesecloth. Lia slipped it over her head and pulled it down. It was tight, fitting her curves snugly, accentuating the shape of her breasts and clinging to the curve of her bottom. It was short, too, coming no more than an inch below her crotch. As she looked down at herself she knew it looked rather slutty, but it was clothing, and nothing gave her more relief than the chance to hide her nakedness.

She combed her hair, then sat down to wait, listening to the throb of the engines and the roll of the ship as it took her far away.

When she heard a key in the door she immediately rose to her feet, smoothing the dress down. The door opened and she found herself facing a man. He was a Hamite dressed in khaki slacks and shirt. He eyed her up and down appreciatively, bringing a new flush of colour to her face.

"Captain waiting," he said. "Come."

Lia followed him out into a narrow corridor. The bulkheads were bare and, like her cabin, pipes ran along below the deck head. On either side were doors, all closed. There was nobody else about.

He led her up three flights of stairs, then along another corridor, stopping outside a door marked *Captain*, on which he knocked.

There was a mumble from inside and the man opened the door and pushed Lia through, closing it behind her. The cabin was much larger than hers, with a carpet and good quality, if rather old furniture. On the bulkheads were pictures of ships, and in one was a porthole through which she could see the night sky.

The Captain was sitting at a table, still dressed in his uniform. On the table was a simple spread of cold meats and salad.

"Come," he said, "sit and eat."

Lia moved nervously across the room and sat down opposite him.

"Eat. Help yourself."

Lia realized she was extremely hungry. She eyed the food with some relish.

"Go ahead. Eat."

The pair ate in silence, Lia relishing the food, momentarily forgetting her situation as she satisfied her hunger. It was only when she pushed away her empty plate that she became aware of the man's eyes upon her.

"Good food?" he asked.

"Yes, thank you."

He leaned forward, gazing into her eyes. "Do you know anything about Hamita?"

"Not very much, Sir."

"Would you like to know?"

Lia thought for a moment. "Yes," she said.

"It is a country of contrasts. In the north, where we are going, it is relatively prosperous and serene. People live good, peaceful lives. There is rule of law and a police force. We would not tolerate those lawless Bikers."

"I see."

"In the south, though, it is different. That part of the country has very little money and, because of that, it is almost ungovernable."

"Why?"

"There is no democracy. The man with the biggest army is in charge. All the time the local tribes fight one another for power."

"Don't they try to take over the north as well?"

"They attack sometimes, but they're always beaten off. The biggest problem is raiding parties. They come in, usually by sea, and steal what they can."

"But the north is more peaceful?"

"Yes. The sort of family that will be interested in you will be a prosperous one. As long as you keep your master happy, then you'll be okay."

"Keep my master happy?"

"The northern Hamites are proud men. They like to believe they give satisfaction to their women. That's what you'll need to learn. You need to show your master you want him. That he brings you pleasure. Not that you are doing what you do because you're forced."

"I... I think I see."

Lia looked across at the man. He was not young, but he had a strong body, and was clearly fit and healthy. She thought about his words. She knew she must learn to fit into her new life, and she sensed he wanted to help her. She knew what she must do.

Tentatively she rose to her feet. She moved around the table until she was standing beside the Captain.

"Master," she said quietly.

"Yes?"

"I... I need you to show me how to bring my new master pleasure."

"I see."

"I want you to instruct me how I should behave."

He eyed her. "All right."

"How should I start, Master?"

"The first thing you should do is make him feel you want him. That you want

106

to give yourself to him. Offer yourself."

Lia stood for a moment, staring into the Captain's eyes. Then slowly, her fingers trembling, she reached up to the straps of her skimpy dress. She slid them down off her shoulders, allowing the material to drop from her firm breasts so that she was naked from the waist up. The Captain sat where he was, his eyes fixed on her as she felt her nipples stiffen under his gaze.

"Master, may I... may I taste you?"

"Taste me?"

"M-may I taste your cock?"

"If that's what you want."

"I want it very much."

"Then you may."

Lia dropped to her knees. She reached out and began to undo his belt. She unbuttoned his trousers, pulling down the zipper and reaching inside.

His cock was sturdy, the helmet smooth and bulbous. Lia licked her lips as she looked at it, suddenly excited at the thought of what she was about to do. She took it in her fingers. It was soft, but already she could feel pulsations. She opened her mouth and took it inside, sucking gently, her tongue licking as she did so. The man gave a muffled groan as she felt it beginning to swell.

A thrill ran through her as she moved her head up and down, her hand caressing his testicles as she fellated him. The taste and scent of a male organ was having its effect on the lascivious girl and, despite her shame at the way she was acting, she felt desire rise inside her as the penis in her mouth reached full erection.

Lia was sucking avidly, her breasts shaking as she concentrated on giving pleasure to the Captain. His cock was throbbing, heightening her excitement as she worked on it.

She let the stiff rod slip from between her lips. She gazed up at him shyly. "Will you fuck me please, Master? I want your cock inside me.'

"It's already been in your mouth. Isn't that enough?"

Lia's cheeks reddened. "No, Master," she said softly.

"Where do you want me to put my cock?"

She lowered her eyes. "I want it inside my cunt."

A slight smile played about his lips. "Take off the dress."

Lia rose to her feet, the dress draped about her hips. She reached down and pulled at it, letting it drop to her feet. She kicked it aside, standing with her legs apart, feeling a trickle of moisture escape from her sex lips as she revealed them to the man.

"Do you masturbate?" he asked.

Lia bit her lip. "Sometimes, Master."

"Masturbate now."

She hesitated for a second, her embarrassment momentarily overtaking her desire. She glanced at the Captain, whose eyes were fixed upon her. Then she let her hand slip down her belly and between her legs.

A small gasp escaped her lips as her fingers found her clitoris, and she began to toy with it, feeling the heat and wetness inside her vagina increase as she did so. She rubbed the hard bud, then slipped a finger between her sex lips. As her desire increased she began to work it back and forth, moaning softly as her passion overwhelmed her.

He knees bent, her hips beginning to gyrate as she slid her fingers in and out, making a wet sound as she did so. Her inner thighs were glistening with moisture, her vaginal fluids coating her fingers.

"Does that feel good?"

"Yes, Master."

"Do you want to give yourself an orgasm?"

She looked at him shyly. "No Master, I want you to do that."

He reached for her arm, pulling her to where he sat. Lia let her fingers drop from her sex. She glanced down at his stiff cock. He held her by the waist and had her straddle his thighs. She spread her legs, giving a soft moan as he lowered her onto his erection.

The sensation of his bulbous cock pressing against her sex lips brought Lia to a new sense of sexual tension. She bit her lip as he pressed her down and penetrated her.

Lia gasped as he pushed deeper and deeper into her, wondering if her vagina could contain this large black rod, feeling the walls of her sex forced open as he pressed inside until at last she was seated on his lap, her vagina filled.

She had been avoiding his gaze, too embarrassed to face him, but he took her chin in his hand and turned her face to his. She felt herself blush as she gazed into his eyes.

"Is this what you want, young lady?"

"Yes, Master. This is what I want."

"Then fuck me."

Lia began to move, lifting herself, then allowing it to come down again, gasping at the sensation of the stout cock that was penetrating her so thoroughly. The man reached for her breasts, squeezing them in his rough hands, bringing fresh gasps of pleasure from the teenager. She fell into a rhythm, moving up and down as she fucked the Captain.

He bent his head forward, closing his lips over hers. Lia let her mouth open as he forced his tongue into it while she pressed herself down onto his rampant cock.

Lia's arousal was reaching its peak, her muscles clenching as she rode the Captain, her breath coming in short gasps.

The man came suddenly, with a grunt of pleasure. As she felt his spunk pumping into her vagina Lia too went over the top, muffled cries escaping her lips as her body convulsed in a shattering climax. The Captain was pressing his hips up as his seed jetted into her.

Lia was overwhelmed by her passion, her naked body shaking as he spent inside her. Then she was coming down, her movements slowing, her heaving breasts easing until finally she was still. Her cheeks aglow with embarrassment at her behaviour, she gazed timidly into his eyes.

"You will be a good slave to someone," he said.

# Chapter 25

For the next few days Lia's life entered a pattern she found almost acceptable. She slept in her cabin, where her meals were brought to her. The porthole cover was removed at the orders of the Captain so she was able to gaze out at the ocean as they progressed. Twice a day she was taken to the rear deck, where she was able to enjoy the air and the sunshine. She was well aware of the lustful glances of the crew members who watched her as she stood in her short dress, enjoying the warm breeze and watching the wake of the ship as they traveled onward, but she knew that under the Captain's orders she was safe from being abused by the crew.

Every evening she was taken to the Captain's cabin for dinner. She was fascinated by his descriptions of life in northern Hamita, of the plush houses and estates of the citizens, and of the sort of place she could expect to live. The Captain's imagery of the living conditions of obedient slaves gave her some relief from the fear she was experiencing as she considered her fate.

Lia's instruction was practical as well, and she found herself offering her body to the Captain in the most shameless ways, allowing him to fuck her in any position he wanted, taking his cock in her mouth, vagina and ass. And, to her intense embarrassment, she found herself revelling in the passions he aroused in her, experiencing multiple orgasms at his hands.

In an odd way she began to love the gruff Captain. Despite the way he used her for sexual gratification, he showed a genuine interest in her welfare, and was clearly concerned that she be equipped to handle her new life. For the first time she could remember Lia found herself enjoying being with her captor, keen to satisfy his desires.

It was the eighth day of the voyage, and Lia was aware it would be their last day at sea. She was in her cabin, in her brief dress, brushing her hair as she awaited the arrival of the seaman who would escort her to the Captain's cabin. She felt an odd pang of sadness that she would be leaving the ship the next day, and she resolved to give the man as much pleasure as she could on their final night.

At first there was no sign that anything was amiss, except that her escort was later than usual in arriving. It was only the sound of a gunshot that made her realize something was wrong.

She ran to the porthole and looked out. As she did so another volley of shots rang out, then a louder explosion. She gazed across the water, then froze with fear. Less than a hundred yards away was another vessel. It was quite a lot smaller than the ship in which she was traveling, a rather shabby boat, its hull stained with rust, but was clearly a lot faster, its bows cutting through the water as it closed in.

It wasn't the speed, or the condition of the vessel that bothered her though. What caught her eye and filled her with apprehension was the large cannon mounted in its bow. Even as she watched the weapon belched fire and smoke, another explosion blasting through the air. Lia heard the ship's engines change note, and guessed the Captain was responding to the threat posed by the gun.

The vessel moved closer, and Lia's heart sank as she saw the deck was lined with swarthy black men carrying rifles. They were pirates! She thought about what the Captain had told her about the southern Hamites and their lawlessness, and she shrank back from the porthole, suddenly afraid.

Within a few minutes the vessels were both stopped, the pirate boat banging against the side of the ship as its men clambered aboard with ropes. Lia wondered what was happening on deck, imagining the crew held at gunpoint. To her relief she heard no more shots, and guessed the pirates were accepting the surrender of the crew.

For the next hour or so she watched as boxes and crates were lowered down the side of the ship onto the deck of the pirate boat, where men hurried to stow them. All the time she listened nervously for footsteps outside her door, but it remained quiet. Indeed, she might well have gone totally unnoticed were it not for one of the pirates dropping a rope over the side of the ship directly outside her cabin.

When she saw the rope against her porthole she wondered for a moment what it was, but then a body slipped down it and she found herself face-to-face with a dark-skinned Hamite with scarred cheeks, his ears decorated with gold earrings. As he caught sight of the girl he stopped, their eyes locked, then Lia backed away, afraid. It was too late; already she could hear the shouts of the man. There was no hiding place in the small cabin. The door was locked. She was trapped.

Minutes passed. Then her heart sank as she heard footsteps in the corridor outside. She listened fearfully as she heard doors being opened and slammed, and the hoarse shouts of men. The noise came closer. Then she saw the handle on her door turn and it crashed open.

She found herself facing four men in dirty jeans and threadbare shirts, with crude tattoos and decorative scars and gaudy gold jewellery. They eyed the girl with undisguised interest, taking in the briefness of her dress and the swell of her breasts.

"What do you want?" said Lia, trying to keep the tremor from her voice. "Th-this is a private cabin."

The men just grinned. Then one stepped forward. "Up on the deck," he ordered.

"Please. This is my cabin. I..."

"Up on the deck!" The man took hold of Lia's arm, his fingers digging into the soft flesh. He thrust her towards the door, where one of the other men caught her and pushed her out into the corridor.

Lia's heart was thumping as she made her way up to the main deck, the three ruffians behind her, shoving her when she showed any sign of lagging.

The sight that met her eyes did nothing to comfort her. On one side of the wide deck stood the Captain, surrounded by his crew. Around them were four pirates bearing rifles. Elsewhere were more pirates, dragging boxes and bags to the side of the ship where they were being loaded onto the smaller vessel. Watching what was happening was a powerful, bearded Hamite, dressed in jeans and a yellow silk shirt. He wore even more jewellery than the other men, and his appearance and bearing made it clear that he was the leader. Lia shuddered as she felt his eyes on her.

The man made a sign to the pirates holding her, and she was marched across to him. He was tall, his shoulders broad, his waist slim. But it was his eyes that caught Lia's attention. Dark, brooding eyes that stared down at her, with a glint of cruelty, making her feel small and helpless.

"Why are you on this ship?"

"P-please, I'm being taken to Hamita."

"A white girl going to our country?"

"Y-yes, Sir."

"For what reason?"

"I..." Lia's voice trailed away.

"Well?"

"I was just visiting."

"Visiting? Don't you know what we think of you people?"

"Sir?"

"The way you treat us as inferiors? The way you imprison us, use us as your slaves?"

"Sir, I didn't..."

"Quiet, little slut. Now tell me, why are you on the ship?"

"What I said is true. I'm being taken to Hamita."

"Are you a whore? The only type of white woman who'd go to our country would be one hoping to sell her body. How much are you selling it for?"

"I-I'm not."

"You have a body worth selling."

Lia stared at him, unable to find a response.

"Let's see what she's got to offer."

He turned to one of the men holding her and nodded. Lia watched fearfully as he drew a long knife from his belt. She tried to shrink back, but the pirates holding her arms were too strong.

The man moved close, staring down into her face. Then he reached out and with two deft movements sliced through the dress. Lia gave a little cry as it fell away, exposing her breasts to those watching. There was a murmur of approval. Lia felt her cheeks redden as the leader examined her breasts, taking in the smooth curves and the darkness of her inviting nipples. Lia realized the exposure was bringing out those desires she strove to suppress, feeling her

111

nipples pucker under the gaze of the men.

"Hmm, I suppose a little whore like you could make some money from the perverts of the north," said the pirate leader. "Come on, let's see the rest of your whore's body."

Lia watched in dismay as the sharp blade slipped between her hip and the dress. Then with a single slash he slit the garment in two. It fell to the deck at Lia's feet, leaving her totally naked. She cringed with embarrassment as she heard the laughter of the watching pirates.

"You don't wear underwear," barked the man.

"I... I don't have any."

"Only a whore has no underwear. Have you no shame either?"

Lia lowered her eyes.

"Open your legs."

"Please I..."

The pirate's broad palm slapped down hard across Lia's bare breasts, wrenching a cry of pain and surprise from the girl.

"Open them!"

Lia bit her lip, fighting back the tears. Then, reluctantly, she moved her feet apart.

"Wider. Display yourself like the whore you are."

Lia did as she was told, the pirates goading her.

"C-can I go back to the crew now?" asked Lia, looking across to where the Captain stood with his men, his face a picture of concern as he witnessed her debasement.

"You want to go fuck with that old man?"

"I... I just want to be with them."

The chief sneered, then moved closer to her. "What do you think we're doing here?" he asked. "Why do you think we're on this ship?"

"To... to rob it, Sir."

"That's right. We're taking everything that's worth money."

Lia felt her heart sink as she took in what he was saying. "You mean..."

"There are perverts out there who will pay a good price for a white girl. A slut like you is worth money."

Filled with dread Lia glanced across at the Captain again. He was looking on, clearly upset about what was happening. She couldn't allow herself to be taken by these brutal men.

Suddenly she snatched her arm from the grip of the pirate holding it, then turned and bit the hand of the man that held her right arm, bringing a cry of pain from him. She lunged forward, pushing the pirate chief, catching him unawares. Then she was running, sprinting across the deck, heading for the side, planning to throw herself into the sea.

She had not gone more than a few paces when something wrapped about her leg, dragging her back, causing her to sprawl onto the deck. A leather whip was wound around her calf, and holding its handle was the pirate chief, his cruel lips curled into a grin as he gazed down at the sprawling figure.

"Thought you could escape, whore? Well, you'll pay for that." He turned to the pirate who was nursing his bitten hand. "Put the bitch onto the boat. Tie her to the yardarm. We'll see how she reacts to the lash."

Lia's pleas fell on deaf ears as the cruel men dragged her across the deck towards the pirate boat.

# Chapter 26

Lia stood, her arms stretched above her head, her legs spread wide, her naked body totally helpless. The men who had dragged her onto the pirate vessel showed no mercy, binding her wrists with coarse rope, then flinging the end over a horizontal boom and pulling, stretching her up on tiptoe, straining the muscles of her arms. Then they tied more rope about her ankles, securing them to a pole that forced her legs wide apart.

When done the pirates stood back, admiring her naked body, her breasts stretched by the tension, her sex open, revealing her labia and clitoris. They lingered briefly, toying with her breasts, pinching the nipples and grinning at her discomfort. Then they probed her pussy, laughing as she groaned, commenting on the wetness there. Lia gritted her teeth, trying to ignore the sensations, but as so often happened her nudity, bondage and helplessness conspired to awaken the perverse desires that lurked deep within her.

The men returned to their duties, leaving the girl to watch as bags and boxes were loaded aboard the boat. All the while the pirate leader was in charge, shouting orders to the men while the Captain and his crew were forced to stand and watch.

At last the pirates seemed to have taken all they wanted, and they began to come back aboard their vessel. The leader too came on board, leaving only three armed men watching the Captain and his crew. He continued to give orders, and when the final item was stashed he made his way across to where Lia hung.

He stood gazing at her, his eyes taking in the swell of her breasts, then dropping to her sex. Lia closed her eyes, wishing she was not naked and on display before the rough men.

"Take a last look at your former masters," said the pirate chief.

Lia glanced across at the ship. The pirate vessel's powerful motors were running, and as she watched they began to pull away from the hull of the ship. She could see the Captain, and the look of concern on his face as he watched her being taken. Lia felt a tear well up in her eyes as she gazed across at him.

"I guess you'll miss being fucked by the old man," said the leader.

Lia glared at him, her heart heavy with despair as the pirate vessel opened its throttles, speeding away from the ship.

"Now there's the matter of your behaviour," went on the chief. "Ndoga, show me your hand."

The man Lia had bitten stepped forward, holding out his hand for the pirate chief to inspect. It had been a hard bite, and blood was still seeping from the wound. The chief glanced at it, then turned back to Lia.

"You have injured one of my men," he said. "For that you must be punished."

Lia felt her stomach tighten. He was still holding the whip, and he grinned as he saw her eyes drop to it.

"You have been whipped before?"

Lia looked at him. "N-not with one like that," she stammered.

"Then we need to let you taste it." He turned to Ndoga. "What do you think? Ten strokes?"

"Yes Chief. Ten is a good number."

A murmur went up from the watching pirates. Lia looked around at them. They were clearly enjoying the spectacle she made. She wondered why fate was so cruel to her. Wherever she went she met cruelty and indifference. She wondered too at her own disposition. Even as she eyed the whip she felt a strange, perverse thrill. How was it possible that in such a situation she could feel her juices flow and her clitoris swell?

The chief moved closer. He ran the handle of the whip up her inner thigh, his eyes fixed upon hers. Lia gave a little gasp as it came in contact with her open vagina. He began to move it back and forth, the leather rasping against her love bud, shivers of lust running through her young body as the pirate stimulated her in front of his crew. Lia tried desperately to ignore what he was doing, but she could feel her hips pressing down against the whip, her nipples hardening as her body responded.

When he pulled the handle away it was smeared with her juices. The chief held it up in front of her face.

"I see this is exciting you, little white slut. Don't worry, you will get what you desire. My crew will see to that."

Lia looked round at the men. All had their eyes fixed on her and she shivered as the meaning of his words sank in.

He moved around behind her, his men standing back. He flicked the whip in the air, the sound bringing fresh apprehension to his young captive. Then he pulled back his arm.

Whack!

The leather came down hard on Lia's bare behind, cutting into her soft flesh and bringing a gasp from her as the stinging pain engulfed her.

Whack!

The second stroke came across the top of her legs, just beneath the swell of her backside, the whip wrapping about her leg.

Whack!

This time the leather sliced into her back, bringing fresh shocks of excruciating pain to the beautiful girl, her body shaken by the force of the blow.

Whack!

The chief was clearly an expert with the whip, each stroke finding a fresh area of pale flesh and marking it with a cruel stripe that darkened to red.

Whack!

Lia was struggling, pulling vainly at the rope that bound her, her naked body twisting in a hopeless effort to avoid the dreadful lash. Around her she could hear the laughter of the men as they watched her twist and turn.

Whack!

A cry of pain escaped her lips as the whip wrapped around her back, the tip catching her nipple with agonizing consequences.

Whack!

The pirate chief's aim with the weapon was unerring, the leather cutting a new weal into Lia's bare ass and wrenching a fresh cry from the girl. Her whole body was on fire, a sheen of perspiration covering her flesh.

Whack!

The man brought the tip of the whip up between her open legs, cutting into the crack of her backside, catching her clitoris, triggering more mocking laughter from the pirates as she cried out in a mixture of pain and lust.

Whack!

Lia was almost out of control, writhing in bondage.

Whack!

The final blow cut into her flesh with tremendous force, thrusting her body forward. Then it was over, the naked girl hanging in her bonds, her face stained with tears. She gasped as she felt the handle of the whip rubbing between her legs, chafing against her swollen clitoris. Instinctively she thrust down against it, her hips jabbing forward as she came with a cry, her juices weeping onto the leather handle as the chief thrust it against her naked pussy, rubbing her roughly while the mob about her shouted and jeered. Lia didn't care, shaking with desire as an orgasm swept through her, bringing wave after wave of passionate pleasure to her. Then she calmed, and the full shame of her behaviour filled her as she realized the wanton sight she made before the scornful pirates.

The chief held the whip handle before her face.

"Clean it. Use your tongue."

Her cheeks glowing Lia began to lick her pussy juice from the weapon, tasting her arousal as she did so. Eventually the chief lowered the weapon, then turned to his men.

"Cut the whore down, and bring her to my cabin."

# Chapter 27

Lia stood in the pirate chief's cabin, her head bowed, her wrists secured behind her by coarse rope. She was still overcome with shame at the way she had responded to the whipping. She could scarcely believe that the cruel punishment had brought her to an orgasm in front of the gang of leering pirates. After the awful penalty she had been cut down and forced to stand naked, her legs still spread wide by the pole tied to her ankles while she was groped by the men, bringing fresh cries of desire as her body responded to their rough caresses. They tied her hands, then removed the pole that spread her legs and pushed her to his cabin, slapping her punished ass and laughing at her as she hurried along.

She stood in the dank cabin, the walls streaked with rust, the bare metal cool beneath her feet. On each side of her stood a burly escort, and before her was the threatening figure of the pirate chief.

"So," he began, "perhaps now you will recognize who is your master."

Lia glanced up at the man in his bright shirt and flashing jewellery, his dark eyes taking in her nakedness. The thought of him as her master was a frightening one, especially after the kind treatment she had received from the Captain.

Slap! The blow across her breast by one of the pirates brought her back to her senses.

"Answer the chief. Who is your master?"

Lia glanced shyly into the chief's eyes. "You are my master," she murmured.

"Speak up!"

"Y-you are my master."

The pirate chief grinned. "Good. You are learning, little slut. Now obey me and it may not be necessary to whip you again. Understand?"

Lia hung her head. "Yes, Sir."

The chief glanced at the two men. "Leave her with me."

Lia saw the two men exchanging grins as they stepped back, then turned to the door, closing it behind them, leaving her alone with their boss. She was feeling extremely uncomfortable under his gaze.

"Sit on the table."

"Sir?"

Smack! He slapped her breast.

"Don't question my orders!"

Lia hurried to the table and lifted herself onto it, the bonds that secured her wrists making it awkward. The metal felt cold against her bottom, and the welts from the whip made her wince in pain.

"Open your legs. Show me your cunt."

"Please Sir, I..."

"Do it!"

Her cheeks glowing, she moved her knees slightly apart.

"Wider."

Reluctantly she obeyed, spreading her legs, only too aware that she was giving him a clear view of her vagina, and the sheen of wetness that coated her nether lips.

The man moved forward, staring down at the red-faced girl. He reached out a hand and placed it on the flatness of her belly, then slid it down. Lia gave a start as she felt his fingers trace the length of her slit. She wanted to close her legs, but dare not.

116

"Look at me."

Shamefacedly Lia looked up into his cold eyes.

He curled his lip. "What kind of a girl lets a stranger touch her in this manner?"

"You are my master," she stammered.

"And you are without shame. Look at you, sitting naked in front of me, your legs spread, your cunt wet with excitement."

He pressed a finger into her vagina, probing her intimately. She gritted her teeth, trying to suppress the sensations of arousal sweeping through her body as he toyed with her pussy. With his other hand he began to fondle her breast, his fingers rolling the nipple between finger and thumb, making it pucker to hardness.

"A good girl would be telling me to stop," he said. "She'd be fighting for her honour. Yet you are getting aroused. You truly are a slut."

Lia didn't answer. She could have pointed out that she was his prisoner, and that she was under threat of punishment, but she knew too that what he was saying was true.

"Get down on your knees," he ordered.

Lia obeyed, her mind a whirl of confusion as she slipped to the cabin floor. Then she was staring at a rigid cock jutting from his jeans.

"You've never tasted Southern Hamite spunk," he said, then thrust his erection into the teenager's face, pressing it against her lips. Meekly she opened her mouth and took his cock inside. She began to suck, wrapping her lips about his shaft, her tongue licking the bulbous glans as he thrust into her. For Lia the taste and scent of male arousal was almost too much, her body alive with sexual tension as she consumed his erection.

The pirate chief showed no consideration for her comfort, grabbing her hair and ramming his penis into her mouth, almost causing her to gag as she fellated him. She sucked greedily, sensing the increase in his arousal. His heavy balls were slapping against her chin as she diligently sucked his cock. He began grunting with pleasure, his groin thrusting against her upturned face as he fucked it with vigour.

He came suddenly, spurt after spurt of semen filling her mouth, trickles of the thick fluid escaping from her lips and dribbling down her chin. She continued to suck, drinking his seed as he went on pumping against her flushed face.

Gradually his movements became less pronounced, his load spent, his thrusts decreasing until, finally, he was still, his cock buried in her mouth as she breathed through her nose. He withdrew, tucking himself back into his jeans while Lia knelt, head bowed.

The pirate leader stood gazing down at her. "Tomorrow morning we dock," he said. "You'll be our figurehead when we come alongside."

She looked up at him, unsure of his meaning.

"We want everyone to see our main prize," he said.

"I... I don't understand."

"You will, soon enough."

# Chapter 28

They had reached Hamita. At first it was a distant strip on the horizon, but as they got closer Lia was able to discern hills and vegetation. Before long the city came into view, its low buildings nestled in a valley. The harbour wall was a grey line and the pirate ship was headed for a gap, with light towers on each side.

As the ship made its lazy passage into the harbour she gazed about, her eyes taking in her new destination. What she saw did not raise her spirits. The sight of the shabby buildings and crumbling docks was an ugly one.

It was a scruffy but busy place, though. On either side of the pirate vessel were rusty trader ships, some idle, some swarming with men. They were working hard, carting cargo on or off the ships while cranes above them creaked and groaned as they lifted and lowered. In the waters of the harbour was a mass of small boats, traveling in all directions. Some were powered by outboard motors, but most were being rowed, by scruffy black peasants. The boats were piled high with all kinds of wares, making them ride dangerously low in the water. Everywhere there was noise, dirt and squalor, and Lia was being taken into the midst of it.

Under any normal circumstances, even if fully clothed, Lia would have felt conspicuous; a white girl among the hoards of native Hamites. But it wasn't just her nakedness and the fairness of her skin that left her feeling more exposed than ever. It was her situation. The pirate chief had her secured to the ship in the most extraordinary manner.

She was in the bow, positioned like some figurehead of an old galleon, secured so she was unable to move. Her arms were tied tight behind her, ropes about her elbows secured to the bowsprit above her, leaving her hanging awkwardly, the coarse rope biting into her. Her legs were stretched wide behind, the ropes that tethered her ankles attached to rings set into the deck.

But it was the final part of the restraint that was the most shameful. A circular pole, about two inches in diameter, had been thrust deep into her vagina, filling her completely. The pole was secured to the ship's deck, leaving her skewered upon it. Thus the young beauty was projected over the front of the pirate vessel, her pert breasts thrust forward, her body on display to anyone in the harbour.

And it wasn't long before the people began to notice her. At first just one or two were gaping, pointing in her direction. Soon cries, whistles and shouts reached her ears as more and more people became aware of the naked white girl in the bow of the pirate vessel as it made its way alongside. Many of the smaller boats were steered towards it, all eyes fixed on the spread-eagled female, her vagina plugged with a wooden pole, which was having a very unwelcome effect on her. Every time the bow rose and fell it would move slightly back and forth inside her. Lia fought to suppress her emotions, but in vain, her clitoris swelling, her love juices leaking as her body reacted to the virtual fucking she was receiving.

The pirates, watching from behind her, let out guffaws of laughter as they sensed her arousal.

Lia gritted her teeth. They were almost at the quayside. The ship was driving in nose first, so that her spread body was coming in over the dock. Workers were swarming around, and as the bow nudged against the tires that lined the wall she found herself suspended a few feet above their heads, the men jumping and trying to touch her body.

The vessel was swinging round as the pirate leader brought it alongside. But Lia was left suspended and exposed for some hours more as the vessel was made fast and unloaded. It was a few hours of torment as men and women came by to stare at her and mock her. Some threw small pebbles, laughing and congratulating one another when they managed to hit her breasts. Others used sticks to poke at her, the coarse ropes biting into her wrists and ankles and the pole in her vagina exciting her in a most unwelcome manner. It was only with extreme effort that she managed to remain in control, fighting down the urge to come, though her nipples remained stiff and sex juice coated the pole.

When at last the pirate chief appeared Lia was close to exhaustion, her naked flesh shiny with sweat. She glanced back at the man as he stood running his eyes over her.

"You make a good figurehead," he mocked. "I almost fancy keeping you there, but it's time to move you on. The slavemaster Darka is here. He'll take you now."

The words filled her with dread.

"There's your new master."

He pointed to a man standing on the dock. He was in his forties and overweight, his stomach bulging. He wore a brightly coloured robe, a pistol in a holster at his hip. He was bald, his ears adorned with gold jewellery. He was accompanied by two scruffy men, both similarly armed and both staring hungrily at Lia's beautiful body. One of them carried a cane.

"Farewell, slut."

The pirate chief drew a curved sword from his belt and sliced through the bonds at Lia's ankles. For a few seconds she was suspended just by her arms, and by the pole that remained embedded in her sex. Then he cut the ropes at her wrists and elbows and with a cry she found herself falling into the water below. It was cool, and for a few seconds she relished the way it enveloped her, washing the sweat from her body and hiding her from the hungry eyes of those watching. Then she was at the surface, gasping for breath as she trod water. She wiped the water from her eyes and looked up at the dock wall.

Momentarily she contemplated escape, thrusting out across the harbour away from the pirate vessel. But as quickly as the thought entered her head she dismissed it. There was nowhere for her to go. Nowhere that the pirates couldn't recapture and punish her. She was theirs now, and she must accept that.

There was a metal ladder that ran up the dock wall, and wearily she paddled across to it and took hold. She climbed slowly, the water running off her naked flesh as she went from rung to rung. Above she could hear the slavemaster shouting, but she blocked it from her mind, trying not to think about what was in store for her.

As her head came above the wall she saw the man standing there, his arms crossed, his two servants on either side of him. Behind him a crowd was gathered, and it was an indication of his stature that they kept a respectful distance. As Lia stepped onto the dock he crooked a finger, indicating that she should approach him. Her immediate desire was to turn and jump back into the water, but instinctive submissiveness took control, and she walked nervously across to where he stood. She wanted to cover herself with her hands, but left them at her sides, exposing herself totally to those watching.

"Hands on head. Open legs."

The guttural voice of the slavemaster's servant made her shiver. He was the one holding the cane. Hesitantly she obeyed, placing her hands behind her head so her breasts were thrust forward, then reluctantly moving her legs apart, aware of the murmur from the crowd as she displayed her body so openly.

"You will let Mister Darka inspect you."

The slavemaster moved close, his sweaty face staring into hers, making her drop her eyes in embarrassment. He reached out a hand, running his fingers down her cheek, then taking hold of her chin. He moved her head from side to side, taking in her lovely face.

He let his hand drop to her breast, closing his fingers on it, caressing and making the nipple stiffen. Lia fought the urge to pull away as the man touched her intimately, too aware of the numerous eyes watching.

He toyed with both breasts, squeezing them, as if examining ripe fruit at a market. Then his hand dropped lower. Lia gave a gasp as a finger traced her slit, seeking her clitoris and teasing it.

"Bend knees."

Lia glanced at the servant who had given the order. Then round at the watching crowd, noticing the way they nudged one another, pointing at her.

Whack!

The cane swept down across her bare buttocks, bringing a cry from her as a stripe etched into her soft flesh.

"Bend Knees."

The man raised his cane again, staring threateningly at the lovely girl. Reluctantly Lia crouched, pressing her hips forward.

The slavemaster gave a brief nod.

"That is how you will present yourself to men in future. Understand?"

"Y-yes." Lia bit her lip as his hand again reached for her sex. It was open to him now, the wetness that coated the lips and clitoris visible to all. She gave a little grunt as he pressed his fingers into her vagina, probing deep. His eyes were fixed on her face, and she knew he was taking in her reaction, watching the lust in her eyes as her body responded.

"You like it when people watch you?"

"I... no. Please, I... oh!" The cry escaped her lips as he twisted his fingers inside her, making her involuntarily press her hips down against his hand and bringing a fresh murmur from the crowd.

He withdrew his fingers, drawing a sigh from the naked girl, her breasts rising and falling as she fought to bring her body under control.

"Clean my fingers."

He held his hand up in front of Lia's face. She stared at the glistening wetness that coated his podgy fingers. Then she leaned forward slightly, her legs still bent, and began to lick her juices from them.

"I can see you have been trained," he said. "I think you will bring me a good price, little white slut."

# Chapter 29

As Lia made her way along the dusty streets of the town she looked neither right nor left, her cheeks glowing with humiliation. The slavemaster had made his men tie her hands behind her, so her naked body was on open display, her breasts quivering with every step. All around her were sneering, chattering people. Clearly it was unusual for a white person to be seen in the Hamite community. For that person to be a girl and totally naked brought even more interest, and the streets were lined with men and women, all taking in her charms, shouting comments as she passed.

The road was hot and stony beneath her bare feet, but Lia was forced to keep pace with her captors. The moment she showed any sign of lagging the cane was brought down across her buttocks, bringing a cry of pain from the unhappy girl and a cheer from those watching. Already she knew her bum was decorated with red stripes, the cane biting into her flesh.

The road twisted up and away from the harbour, and she found herself walking through a busy town with small shops, the vendors standing in the doorways shouting their wares. Women carrying heavy baskets on their heads would pause and watch her pass, their expressions filled with contempt as they took in her appearance.

A gob of spit struck her breast, dribbling down over her nipple, provoking fresh cries of contempt from those watching. Lia tried her best to close her mind to those around her as she trudged on through the shabby streets, but it was impossible to ignore the shouts and derision to which she was exposed.

They turned a corner and ahead she could see a tall dark building. Like all the others it was badly in need of repair, the stones worn and dirty. But it was the windows that caught her eye. They were small, set high in the wall with rusting bars across them. Behind them she thought she could glimpse dark faces, and she shivered as she contemplated who was staring down at her.

Attached to the building was a high wall, its top decorated with barbed wire.

There was a heavy metal door in the wall, and Lia realized she was being led to it. Her escorts pulled her to a halt outside the door and one of them banged on it.

"Mister Darka is here!" he shouted.

At first nothing happened. Then a small slit opened and Lia saw a pair of eyes staring out. Moments later came the sound of a key grinding in a heavy lock, and the door creaked open.

The man inside was dressed in jeans, like the others, but he wore a khaki jacket with stripes on the sleeves. On his chest was a threadbare badge that had the words *Prison Warder* on it. He carried a rifle.

"Criminal?" he asked.

Darka shook his head. "One of mine."

The man nodded. "A slut for fucking. Where she from?"

"Delivered today. She's coming inside."

The guard stood aside as the escort thrust her through the opening, his companion and Darka following them. The door creaked shut again and the guard turned the key in the lock.

"She to go to Mister Darka's block?" asked the guard.

"Yes."

"Better get her processed then."

"Sure." Darka's man shoved Lia forward. "Get moving. Over there."

Lia looked about as she walked. She was in a large yard. The ground was crumbling concrete and all around were the high walls and barbed wire. It was a prison. But she had committed no crime. Darka's words *one of mine* went through her head. It seemed the man had friends in high places if he was allowed to keep his slaves in a prison.

Her captors were directing her to a door in the side of the building. Like the one by which she had entered, it was large and made of rusty metal. As they got closer it swung open and she found herself facing another scruffy prison officer, who grinned as he studied the helpless girl.

"Mister Darka, you find a good one there I think."

Darka grunted.

Lia hesitated, only to get another swipe across her bare backside with the cane.

"Get inside, bitch."

She stepped through and found herself in a long bare corridor, the floor concrete, the walls painted a dull grey. She was pushed forward towards a barred door. The guard unlocked it, then she was inside.

The room into which she was taken was almost circular in shape, with barred doors all around it, each one leading into a corridor where more barred doors were visible. In the centre was a large desk, behind which sat more men in tatty uniforms. There was a musty smell in the air, and the floor clearly hadn't been swept for ages. Lia shivered slightly as she absorbed the atmosphere of the awful place.

122

Her escorts pushed her up to the desk, where a fat balding man sat. He eyed her up and down with interest.

Whack!

The cane swept across Lia's backside, making her yelp and jump.

"How do you stand?"

She quickly moved her legs apart, bending her knees and pressing her hips forward to take up the humiliating stance she had been instructed to use.

The man behind the desk ran his eyes up and down her body. "One of yours, Mister Darka?"

"Yes."

"Okay. We'll process it."

"Good. I'll be back tomorrow."

"Anything special?"

"Just let her know that obedience is required."

"Don't worry."

One of Darka's men moved behind Lia and unfastened her wrists, though having done so a pair of cold handcuffs took the place of the rope, pinning her arms again. Lia watched as her new master and his men were led out through the barred door, then turned to face the man behind the desk.

"You heard what Mister Darka said. Obedience."

"Yes Sir."

He turned to one of the prison guards. "Take it to processing."

"That way," the guard barked, pointing at one of the doors. He gave her a shove that sent her staggering towards it. Another officer swung it open. Lia went through, receiving a slap on her bum as she did so. Again she found herself in a dank corridor with doors on either side.

She was forced to hurry along the corridor.

"Stop!"

She found herself outside another door. There was a sign on it, but in a language she didn't understand. The guard banged on the door. It swung open and she was confronted by a man in a long white coat. He had thinning hair. On his coat was a badge that said *Nkasi*. He eyed the naked girl with interest.

"Mister Darka's property," said the guard.

The man nodded. "Why else would a female be in this place? Bring her in."

Lia received a shove in the back, pushing her into the room. She looked around. There were three other men in the room, lounging behind desks, their eyes fixed on her. Her cheeks glowing she spread her legs and thrust her hips forward as she had been instructed, causing the men to smirk.

"Okay," said Nkasi, "leave her with us."

The guard headed for the door, closing it behind him as he left. Nkasi then indicated the desk to her left. "Over there," he said.

Lia moved, taking up her demeaning pose in front of it. The man facing her had an expression of amusement on his face as he looked her up and down.

Questions were barked in quick succession, with Lia answering in timid tones as the man scribbled on a form. At first they were what she'd expect, like name and age, but then they became more personal.

"Are you a virgin?"

"N-no."

"How old were you when you were first fucked?"

"Sir?"

He banged his fist on the desk. "How old?"

"S-seventeen, Sir."

"How many sexual partners have you had?"

"I... I don't know."

"Come on, answer the question," said Nkasi. "How many men have you fucked?"

"I really don't know, honestly."

"Fifty? A hundred? Two hundred?"

"I'm not sure."

"Maybe more than that?"

"I don't know."

"Put down two hundred."

The man at the desk scrawled the number, a smile on his face as he eyed her up again.

The questions went on. Lia knew they were toying with her, embarrassing her still further, as if being naked was not enough. At last they declared themselves done with the questions, but her relief was short-lived as they moved her on to the second desk.

"Stand straight."

The man rose to his feet, holding a tape measure. He began measuring her body, allowing his hands to roam over her naked flesh as he wrapped the tape about her, caressing her breasts and probing her sex with his fingers as he worked, bringing an unwelcome sense of arousal to the girl as she responded to his touch, to the obvious amusement of those watching.

Lia was ordered in front of the third desk. The man behind it pulled on a white coat and draped an old stethoscope about his neck.

"Now you must be medically examined," he said.

Lia didn't believe he was a doctor.

"Over there. Get on the table."

It was metal and cold, painted dark green.

"Lie on your back," he instructed.

Knowing she had no choice, Lia obeyed. She shivered slightly as she gazed up at the ceiling.

"Open your mouth."

She did as she was told. The man began probing inside, running his fingers over her teeth and pressing her cheeks out. Then his fingers moved lower, taking her breasts and kneading them, making the nipples harden. The other men gathered round to watch.

"Open your legs."

Lia parted her thighs, giving the men an unrestricted view of her sex.

"Bend your knees. Lift your hips."

Her cheeks glowing she did as she was told, raising her bottom off the table.

The man moved his hand down to her inner thigh, stroking her soft flesh and bringing an unwelcome pulse of arousal to her.

He moved his hand back, tracing the lips of her sex. Lia struggled to control her emotions as her body responded to his intimate touch.

Fingers sought her clitoris. She groaned softly, her hips beginning to move as he caressed her there, then suddenly he slapped her inner thigh, making her yelp.

"Get to your feet. I'm done with you."

For a second Lia lay where she was, confused by the way the man was treating her, and by her response. Then as he raised his hand to slap her again she scrambled from the table.

"Get over there. Identification time." Nkasi indicated a bare wall where a fourth man was standing, holding a camera. Lia moved across, fighting the arousal the man's touches had stirred.

"Hold this and stand against the wall." The man handed her a small board on which numbers were written. "Hold it in front of you, where I can see it. Come on, face me."

Reluctantly Lia stood with her back to the wall and stared into the camera lens, holding the numbered board a few inches under her chin.

The shutter clicked a few times.

"Turn sideways. That's it. Now the other way. Good. Job done."

# Chapter 30

It was loud banging on her cell door that brought Lia to her senses with a start. She had been dreaming of happier times, when she was servant to Thorkil, the Biker who rescued her from Helda and treated her with compassion. In her dream she was wearing an elegant dress, sparkling jewellery decorating her body as she danced with the Biker in a beautiful ballroom. Now, opening her eyes, her heart sank as she took in the bare walls of her cell, and knew she was lying naked on a stained mattress on the floor.

She'd lost count of how many days she had been at the prison, but she guessed it was at least two weeks. It had been a gruelling time for her.

After her processing, she had begged to be allowed to wear prison garments The clothes the prisoners wore were grey and worn, but at least they provided a degree of modesty. But she received no more than a dismissive snort of laughter from Nkasi.

"Those uniforms are for the criminals," he said. "You are Mister Darka's property. They wear their own clothes."

"But I don't have any clothes."

"That is because you are a shameless slut. So shameless you shall remain."

She had been led from the processing room along more corridors, deep into the prison. On the way they passed through a number of cell blocks where the prisoners lined the bars, calling out explicit crudities to the naked beauty as she passed, her hands cuffed behind her, her breasts shaking deliciously with every step she took.

Darka's wing was a small one, on one of the upper floors. It was guarded by men in green uniforms that set them apart from the other prison guards. Lia was handed over to the men by the prison guards, enduring their lewd taunts, standing quietly while they commented on her breasts and pussy and ass. Then the prison guards left, and Lia was led through yet another prison door into Darka's wing.

She found herself in a long dingy room with cell bars running down either side. The cells themselves were divided by bars running from floor to ceiling, giving no privacy whatsoever. There were about half a dozen other prisoners in the block, all men and all wearing tattered clothes. They appeared weary with captivity, although all showed some interest when the naked white girl was brought into their midst.

Lia was led to a cell halfway along. Her handcuffs were removed and she was pushed inside. The cell had a single hard-backed chair, a mattress and a bucket. The key was turned in the lock, and she was a prisoner once again.

From then on the days passed slowly. Lia had nothing to do but sit and contemplate her fate, surrounded by staring men. They were clearly not Hamites. Whilst black men, their skin was much darker than that of their captors. They were taller, with angular features, their hair worn in braids. Lia was to learn that they were Nilotes, from a neighbouring country which had an ongoing border dispute with the Hamites for many years.

The one thing the men shared with the Hamites, though, was their obvious interest in the girl. They would chat amongst themselves, gesturing in her direction. The men in the cells on either side of her would beckon her to come close to the bars, their arms reaching out for her, so she was forced to stay well away. They would pull out their cocks, calling to her to watch as they masturbated. Often Lia would jump as semen was projected at her, spattering her naked flesh, bringing a cheer from the watching men.

They would watch her as she performed her ablutions, squatting over the bucket amid their shouts and goading. Once a day a bucket of cold water and soap was brought to her cell and she was obliged to wash herself under the eyes of the other prisoners.

The one bit of relief was that she was not molested while in the cells. She had expected the guards to use her body at will, such was her vulnerability, but Darka clearly had control over them. They would occasionally bring other guards to stare at her, ordering her into provocative poses while they watched, but they never actually touched her.

And now something was happening. It was barely dawn, a soft light showing through the small window of her cell. Lia wiped the sleep from her eyes and rose unsteadily to her feet. The cell block was unusually busy, with guards bustling about and shouting orders. Some of the other cell doors were open, and the occupants were standing whilst heavy metal shackles were used to trap their hands behind them.

A guard at Lia's door unlocked it, and strode into the cell. "Turn around."

The confused girl obeyed, and felt her arms pulled back as cold metal closed about her wrists. Then the guard turned her to face him and a collar, also made of rough metal, was fastened around her neck, locked with a stout padlock. The man paused for a moment, closing his hands over her bare breasts, his face spread in a grin. Then another guard, clearly senior to him, snapped an order and he ceased his caresses, taking Lia by the shoulder and pushing her to the door.

Her fellow prisoners were in a line, their collars fastened one to the next by stout chains. She was pulled forward and her collar attached to the man in front of her. Then she felt another chain attached to the back of her collar as the next prisoner was placed in the line.

Another order was shouted, and the gate to the block was swung open with a clang. Then the line of prisoners was pushed forward.

Lia's mind was a whirl as she found herself being marched through the corridors of the prison once again, this time with the tall Nilotes in front and back of her. They were led down a flight of stairs, then through another heavy door into the prison yard. She recognized the main gate through which she had been brought so many days before, and a shiver ran through her as she saw it was being opened.

The thought of once again being forced to walk the busy public streets completely naked made her heart sink. It seemed that humiliation was to be her destiny in this unfriendly country. But she was in their power now, and had no choice but to do as she was told. With her eyes lowered, Lia followed the man in front of her out into the street.

She had hoped it would at least be quiet at that time in the morning, and her heart sank further as she saw the streets were full of people, obviously on their way to work. As the line of prisoners filed out onto the street she heard shouts of derision hurled at the Nilote men, followed by peals of laughter as they caught sight of the naked white girl sandwiched between them. Once again Lia tried to close her mind to the faces all around as she padded along, but the shame of her situation was never far from her mind as she listened to the taunting.

The guards led them up a long wide road that seemed to be leading to the centre of the town. It was a dirt road, full of bumps and potholes, the stones and grit biting into Lia's bare feet as she walked. It was clear it was not a rich area. The people walked or rode bicycles, and the few vehicles they encountered were battered and rusty. Most of the people were poorly dressed, and the only people she saw who were in any way smartly dressed were men in dark suits who stood and watched the prisoners pass, their eyes hidden behind sunglasses. Lia eyed them nervously. They looked menacing, their suits showing a bulge which she suspected hid a weapon. She noticed too that the people steered clear of these men, stepping into the street where they blocked the sidewalk. Altogether it did not look to Lia to be a safe place. She knew that under normal circumstances, even fully clothed, she would not have walked these streets. To be doing so naked was something she didn't want to think about.

They walked on. There were four guards escorting them, two carrying rifles, the others armed with long sticks that they occasionally used to make them move faster. Lia, in particular, was singled out by them and time after time she felt the canes bite into her bare behind, stinging dreadfully and making her jump, much to the amusement of those watching. Ahead loomed an austere building, with wide stone steps leading up to an impressive entrance with tall stone pillars. Lia saw the word MARKET across the portico, and dread gripped her.

Despite its impressive frontage the building was in a state of disrepair, like most of the town. The steps were chipped and broken, the pillars discoloured, with ivy growing up the walls. People were standing and sitting on the steps, many of them dressed in rags, although the dark-suited men were there as well.

They were driven up the steps by their guards, and at the top was a large doorway, the wooden doors open wide. They were herded inside, into a huge hall full of market stalls. The counters were spread with food. Some held vegetables; skinny carrots, wrinkled tomatoes and soggy cabbages. Others had meat and fish, the odour of which was not at all pleasant. And all around was a cacophony of noise as people bartered with the stallholders.

The motley line of captives was led through the crowd to the far end of the building. Lia could see a platform, set about ten feet above the floor. Ahead was a barred door, and as they approached it was swung open by a guard dressed in the same uniform as their escorts. The prisoners were led through it, into a dark passage with stone walls. It opened into a circular chamber with barred windows set high in the walls.

Lia was glad to be away from the staring crowds, but she felt uneasy as she stared about the foreboding chamber.

The crumbling stone walls were set with metal rings, from which hung heavy chains. Above each ring was a number painted by hand in fading white. In front of each ring was a stone slab about three feet high.

The Nilote at the front of the group was unshackled, then driven across the room by one of the guards, shouting orders and waving his cane. He was directed to go to the slab with the number one above it. More shouting and wielding of the cane saw him climb onto the block and turn to face the centre of the room. The guard then climbed up beside him and fastened the chain that hung from the ring to the back of his collar. He removed the manacles from the man's wrists, then jumped down. The second Nilote was then herded across the room to the second ring.

Lia stood nervously watching as each of the men in front of her was secured. Then it was her turn, the guard shouting incomprehensible orders as he unfastened her from the man behind, then slashed the cane down hard across her bare backside as she scurried across to the wall.

She climbed up onto the platform and stood passively while the man fastened her to the ring. The chain was short, forcing her to stand up straight to avoid strangling herself. Once she was secure the guard removed her cuffs, then tapped his cane against her inner thighs, indicating that she was to move her feet apart. Once she did so to his satisfaction he indicated that she was to place her hands on her head. Then he moved on to the next prisoner, leaving Lia alone and exposed in the strange and frightening place.

# Chapter 31

For the next hour or so Lia was obliged to stand on the small stone plinth, staring across the room at her fellow captors and wondering what fate was about to befall her. The place was clearly a slave market, and she and the men were being put up for sale by Darka. The four guards remained with them, lounging on chairs by the door. Now and then they would get up and wander about the room, occasionally taking a swipe at one or other of the prisoners with their canes.

Eventually voices reached the room and the guards sprang to their feet. The door creaked open, and her heart sank as people began to file in. They were clearly not the ragged citizens from out in the streets. They were all men and dressed in smart clothes, many in traditional robes with jewellery about their necks. Accompanying each were the men in dark suits, two or three with each, glancing suspiciously at the guards. They were clearly bodyguards, to protect the rich men.

She stood still, her gaze fixed in front of her, as the buyers began to move about the room. Most seemed interested in the male prisoners, eyeing them up and down, barking orders to the guards who would open the men's shirts to show their chests, or roll up their sleeves and make them flex their muscles.

But there were some who were interested in the beautiful white girl, and she began to feel very conspicuous as they came to look at her. Most of them were amused at her predicament, pointing at her and passing comments she couldn't understand, but which were obviously filled with derision. Most of them, though, would move on to examine the other captives, obviously having no use for a female.

But it wasn't long before one of the buyers showed interest in Lia. He was a portly man wearing a long colourful robe, and a turban. Around him gathered four of the ominous bodyguards, their eyes hidden by sunglasses. He stood in front of the naked captive, his eyes traveling over her lovely curves. There was another man with him, wearing a plain robe and clearly in his employ. They talked as they eyed her, and Lia feared what was being said.

The turbaned man shouted across to one of the guards. The man hurried across to where he was standing. More words were exchanged, the guard climbed up onto the slab, took hold of her collar and detached the chain, then jumped down again. Lia stood, her hands still clasped upon her head, her legs spread, wondering what was required of her.

"Turn around."

It was the man in the plain robe who spoke, the first words in English she'd heard since leaving the prison. Her cheeks burning, she obeyed.

"Legs wider. Bend forward."

Lia did as she was told, only too aware of the view she was presenting.

"Spread your ass cheeks."

She reached back and pulled her buttocks apart, presenting the men with a perfect view of her most private parts. She gasped as something hard and cold touched her clitoris.

She glanced over her shoulder and saw that one of the bodyguards had a cane, using it to press against her love bud, generating unwelcome shivers of excitement in her, running the wood over her sex lips, then pressing it into her vagina.

Lia struggled to maintain control as she felt the stiff rod penetrate her. The man was pushing it deep, twisting it as he did so. She knew how wet she was, and that the men would see it. Still she held her cheeks apart, a soft moan escaping her lips as the man began to move the cane back and forth inside her.

"You see that she is a willing slave."

Lia recognized Darka's voice. He had joined the men behind her.

"Does she fuck willingly?"

"Certainly. Would you like to see her?"

"Yes. Show me."

The cane was removed, dragging a fresh gasp from her.

"Stand up. Turn around."

This time it was Darka giving the orders and she hurried to obey, facing the men once more, her legs spread, her hands behind her head. She watched anxiously as he gave an order to one of his guards, who turned to the tall Nilote on the slab next to Lia's.

He was freed from his shackles too, and looked confused as he was ordered to climb down, then driven to where Darka was standing with his prospective customers.

Darka looked the man up and down, then spoke a few words to him that Lia couldn't understand. There was no mistaking the look of surprise that crossed the man's face.

Darka turned to Lia. "These men want to see your skills," he said. "They want to be sure you are the shameless little slut I told them you were. They want a demonstration. Do not disappoint them, or me..."

Lia's eyes widened as she looked at the Nilote, then back to Darka. "You want me to...?"

"Yes. Arouse him. Now."

Lia stared back at the Nilote. He was towering over her, his arms muscular, his stomach flat.

"Arouse him."

All eyes turned in Lia's direction, as more of the buyers moved across to watch what was happening. The young beauty shivered as she realized what was required of her. Slowly she moved closer to the slave, then dropped to her knees, careful to keep her legs spread.

Tentatively she reached out and ran a hand over the front of the man's tatty jeans. She undid the button and slid down the zipper. Then she reached inside. He wore no underpants and she gasped as her fingers closed around his penis. It was very large, even in its flaccid state, and she could feel it hardening and growing. She looked up into his face, and saw his desire.

She pulled his cock out, then looked up at Darka, who gave a slight nod. Slowly she leant forward and, opening her mouth, took him inside.

A murmur went up from the onlookers as they watched the white girl sucking the penis in her mouth, her hands caressing the slave's balls as she did so. Lia knew they must think her a shameless whore, but she knew too that she had no choice. But as well as the shame there was another emotion stirring inside her The taste of the man was awakening her own desires. The taste of an erect cock was bringing her perverse desires to the fore, desires increased by her latent exhibitionism as she considered the sight she must make, kneeling naked on the stone and sucking the stranger in so public a place.

"Enough!" said Darka. "Lie on the slab and spread your legs."

Lia let the large cock slip from her lips, but was unable to resist the temptation to lick the man's swollen glans before rising to her feet and lying across the cold slab. She opened her legs, bringing fresh comments from those watching as they perceived the wetness leaking from her vagina. Her fellow slave moved closer and she reached out and took hold of his cock once more, suddenly anxious to feel it inside her.

She guided his erect penis down to the lips of her sex, raising her hips in a blatant display of desire, a groan escaping her as she felt his smooth tip press against her pussy lips.

"You see how she wants it," remarked Darka to his prospective customers. "A true willing whore."

The men nodded in agreement.

The slave began to press his erection forward and her sex opened, allowing him to slide into her, bringing fresh groans of arousal from the girl. She wanted him, needed him, and the sensation of his cock entering her, stretching the walls of her sex, was almost too much. As he buried himself fully inside her, his pubic hair pressing against her clitoris, an orgasm suddenly coursed through her, making her cry out as her body writhed under him.

Then he was thrusting into her, his powerful hips shaking her body as he fucked her. Lia moaned with passion as she felt her desires increase anew, her head rolling from side to side, her breasts quivering enticingly as she responded to her lover.

His hands closed on her bare breasts, his thrusts increasing, his breath coming in pants as he rutted against her. His passion brought new thrills to the naked beauty as she writhed and gasped beneath him. She knew the men watching were aware of how aroused she was, but she was no longer in control of her emotions as the man's thick cock drove deep into her.

Then, with a grunt, the man was coming, and a scream escaped Lia's lips as she felt herself filled by surging semen, a fresh orgasm coursing through her, her hips thrusting up against the man's, her breasts trembling, her nipples erect.

The man emptied his balls into her, his teeth gritted as his orgasm went on. At last, though, he was slowing. He was done, sliding his erection from her and straightening up. As the guard led him back to his platform Lia remained where she was, her breasts rising and falling as she fought to regain her breath, a flow of semen leaking from her open vagina onto the cold hard slab.

Darka turned to his prospective customers.

"So you see," he said. "She will make a more than willing sex slave."

# Chapter 32

Lia watched apprehensively as the tall Nilote slave was taken down from his slab next to hers and led to the door. The auction had been going on for some time now, and with him taken to the sale, she would be next.

It had been a harrowing day for her as more and more men came to view Darka's wares. To her deep embarrassment she had been made to demonstrate her talents a further three times, each with a different Nilote prisoner. Two fucked her lying on her back on the slab, like the first, and the other took her from behind, thrusting his cock into her rear passage. And Lia's reaction had been shameful, orgasms shaking her as she reacted with instinctive passion. Now the prospective buyers all knew what she was capable of, and how easily she could be used and manipulated.

She shivered as she considered what was to come. She had been sold before, to Helda, but this was different. At the club men just used her for their own amusement, these people despised her because of her race, and she knew she would suffer for that. They also looked down on her because of her behaviour, something she was unable to control.

The door opened again and two guards came through, heading for where she stood. Lia watched as they approached, fear running through her naked body. One climbed up on the platform. He undid the chain attached to her collar and pulled her hands behind her, snapping handcuffs onto her wrists. Then he fastened a lead to her collar and passed it to his colleague. The man pulled, forcing Lia to jump from the slab.

The men headed for the door, one pulling her along, the other using his cane to beat her bottom when she showed any sign of reluctance. She could hear voices ahead, and knew she would soon be on open view in the market

They passed through another barred door into a corridor that sloped upward. Ahead she could see a bright light and hear the voices even more clearly. Instinctively she tried to hang back, but the guard tugged harder on the lead, forcing her along while his companion aimed another swipe at her buttocks.

The passage opened into a wide open area and Lia's heart sank as she heard a cheer go up. They had emerged onto a raised platform, below which was the market square, thronging with people, all staring up at her. Lia wished desperately for some clothing, although her nipples puckered to hardness as her exhibitionist tendency came to the fore.

One guard removed her handcuffs and collar, then pushed her to a wooden table. "Climb up. Stand on this."

Her cheeks burning, Lia climbed onto the table. She turned and faced the crowd, spreading her legs and placing her hands behind her head. A fresh cheer came from the crowd as they saw her submissiveness.

A man came forward. He was dressed in a long white robe and was clearly the auctioneer. In his hand he held a gavel and he pointed it at the young beauty. He began to talk, his voice loud and resonant. He was clearly describing her charms, indicating the firmness of her breasts, the curve of her hips and her shapely legs. He pressed the handle of his gavel against her vagina, briefly teasing her clitoris and pointing at the semen marks on her legs. All the time his audience was with him, laughing and cheering his remarks. For Lia it was totally humiliating, yet she had no choice but to stand as her naked body was described in detail.

At last the man turned away from her and made his way across to a battered old lectern that stood to the side of the table. Then the auction began.

Lia watched in trepidation as the hands went up on the floor below her. There were about half a dozen smartly dressed men who were clearly bidding for her. The auctioneer barked out the bids, pointing from one man to another as they raised their hands. Lia had no idea what was being said, or how much the men were offering, but soon there were just two men bidding. One was the first who had examined her, and as she watched he made the final bid. The auctioneer looked at the other man, but he shook his head. Then the gavel came down.

Lia had been sold.

# Chapter 33

"Stand there!"

The guard pushed Lia across to the centre of the room, where she took up her submissive stance, her legs spread, her hands once again cuffed behind her.

It was an hour or more since the auction ended. An hour or more in which she had been kept in a small damp cell with no furniture and only a barred window set high in the wall for illumination. Around her, in similar cells, were her fellow prisoners. They had an air of depression as she sensed them considering their situations, all sold to new masters. It was almost a feeling of relief for her when the guard came to take her away. She found herself in a large office, a desk at one end where a clerk sat scribbling in a ledger.

The door opened, and Lia recognized her new master and his bodyguards. The portly man walked across and eyed her up and down. Lia stayed stock still, staring ahead, trying not to catch his eye. The man gave a slight nod, then walked to the desk.

For the next ten minutes he remained with the clerk, who filled in forms and wrote in his ledger. It was clear that this was the act of purchase, and she was now owned by the Hamite. When he finally finished he stood up and shook hands with the clerk. Then he shouted an order to one of his men.

The bodyguard came close to Lia, reaching into his pocket and pulling out a chain lead. He moved behind her and clipped it onto her handcuffs. Then he slipped it between her legs. He walked back in front of her and took hold of the chain again, giving it a sharp tug. Lia gasped as it pressed against her sex, parting the lips and rubbing against her clitoris. The man saw her reaction, and pulled again.

His boss shouted an order and the bodyguard indicated that Lia was to follow him, tugging on the chain again.

Lia found herself back in the market place. The sale had ended, but there were still a lot of people milling about amongst the trade stalls. The men led her through the throng and into the open air, bringing a new sense of humiliation to her as she found herself naked in the busy streets again.

Parked at the bottom of the steps was an old truck, its tires bald, its paintwork rusty. Lia was led to the back of the vehicle, and a whack on her backside told her she was to climb aboard. With her hands bound behind her she couldn't see how she would manage it, then a pair of strong hands cupped the cheeks of her backside and hoisted her up, sending her sprawling into the back. Moments later one of the men was beside her, dragging her to her feet. He took hold of the chain, produced a padlock and proceeded to fasten it to a ring on the side of the truck. Lia was forced to stand, her hands fastened behind her, her sex lips parted by the chain as the people around looked on.

One of the guards sat on the platform whilst two others climbed into the cab. Then the engine spluttered into life and the truck moved off through the streets.

Lia found she had to place her feet apart in order to maintain her balance as the old vehicle lurched and bounced. She felt terribly exposed standing where she was, an object of amusement and derision from the passers-by who stared up at her. Yet even in such a mortifying situation, the pressure of the chain was bringing fresh arousal to the naked girl as it rasped against her clitoris. Every time the vehicle rocked through a pothole a moan escaped her lips as she thrust down against the chain that bit into her vagina. To make matters worse, the truck frequently came to a halt while the driver spoke to people at the side of the road. The people would gather round, the men laughing and pointing, the women glaring at her. Somehow the exposure increased the lustful feelings in the naked girl, her exhibitionist tendencies bringing a surge of lust as she thrust her hips down against the chain.

They were stopped amid a crowd when she came at last, a cry escaping her lips as she ground her hips down, making the chain rasp back and forth over her swollen clitoris as her juices seeped from her vagina. The people shouted their derision as they realized she was having an orgasm, some of the women contemptuously spitting at her as the truck began to move off again.

The shame of her behaviour overcame the girl, and she fought down her desires, trying to stand so that the pressure of the chain was reduced. Still she knew she had acted shamefully and she couldn't look into the face of the guard sitting beside her.

They drove for about half an hour, reaching the outskirts of the city, turning down a rough dirt road riddled with potholes. At last they stopped behind a pair of high gates. The driver sounded his horn and the gates were pulled open. Then they proceeded up a driveway to a large house, an old colonial building with wide steps running up to the front door. Like most buildings in this country it was somewhat rundown, but it was clearly owned by someone important, as the black Mercedes outside revealed. All around was a high fence beyond which were fields of crops with, here and there, the sight of a scruffy Nilote working. Lia wondered for a moment if she had been bought as a farm worker. That at least would be tolerable. She wasn't afraid of doing honest toil. But she knew in her heart that was not the case. She had been bought for her body.

The guard unlocked her lead. He pushed her off the trailer onto the dirt driveway. Then he grabbed her lead again and pulled her towards the house.

They did not go up to the main door. Instead she was led around the back of the house to a servant entrance. Led inside, Lia found herself in a narrow corridor. She was taken down it, then pushed through a door into a small room. It was almost bare of furniture, with just a single chair by the window.

The guard shouted something, and moments later two young girls appeared. They were Hamites of a similar age to Lia and both wore maid's costumes. When they caught sight of the naked white girl they stopped short, giggling.

The guard spoke again, his voice stern. The two young women stopped giggling and nodded obediently. The guard looked Lia up and down once more, then left the room.

The girls turned to her.

"You slave girl," said one of them. She was as petite as Lia, her hair cropped short, her eyes large. On her apron was clipped a badge with the name Shuba.

"Yes, you do as we say," put in the second. She was taller, her hair tied back. Her badge bore the name Laska.

Lia looked at the pair. They were obviously very junior servants in the house, yet they clearly considered themselves superior to her. She was beginning to understand how isolated and degraded the Hamites felt in her own country.

The girls stared down at the chain, still lodged between Lia's legs, the lips of her vagina holding it there. They nudged one another and giggled afresh.

"White girls like that?" asked the one called Shuba. "You like a chain there?"

"Looks like she likes men's cocks there as well," put in Laska, pointing at the trails of semen down Lia's legs.

"Come, dirty white girl. Time to clean you up."

Laska took hold of the lead, tugging it. Lia was forced to follow the two maids out of the room and down the corridor again. They took her through a door that led into a bathroom. By one wall was an old bathtub on small legs. Shuba turned on the large faucets, causing water to gush into the tub.

As her companion filled the bath Laska undid her manacles, freeing Lia's hands. "No need to take your clothes off," she giggled.

"Where are your clothes?" asked Shuba.

"I don't have any," said Lia, bringing fresh laughter from the maids.

"You don't have any?"

"Dirty little white girl. Get in the bath."

Gingerly Lia climbed over the side. The water was lukewarm, making her shiver, but she was glad of the opportunity to clean herself.

Shuba knelt down beside the bath, a cake of soap in her hand. To Lia's surprise she began to wash her.

"She feel good?" said Laska.

"Soft," replied her companion, running her hands over Lia's breasts, squeezing as she soaped them.

"You are making her nipples stiff," said Laska. "You think she is like you?"

"A girl who prefers other girls?" said Shuba. "Could be. I think she is liking this."

The maid moved her soapy hand lower, running it over Lia's belly. Then she was seeking her vagina, fingers probing.

"You like being touched here?"

Lia didn't reply, but she found herself spreading her legs wider as the black maid's fingers probed intimately. Lia wondered at her desires. The feel of the young maid's fingers was something she couldn't ignore, and she found her breath shortening as the maid toyed with her clitoris.

"White girl is excited," said Laska.

Her companion laughed. "But I prefer black girl."

With that she withdrew her fingers from Lia's vagina, leaving her gasping slightly as she brought herself back under control. The girl continued to wash her, soft hands moving over her naked flesh. At last she was finished, and the aroused girl was ordered to climb from the tub.

The two maids towelled her body, Laska working on her back while Shuba dried her front, fingers lingering on Lia's breasts and sex, bringing sighs from the naked girl.

They ran combs through Lia's hair, then stood back to admire her shapely form. A bell rang.

"The master wants you," said Shuba. "Come."

"C-couldn't I have some clothes?"

Smack! Laska brought her palm down hard on Lia's bare backside.

"No talking without permission. You will do as we say." She opened the door and gestured for Lia to follow her.

# Chapter 34

As Lia walked along the corridor between the two young maids she pondered her fate. Once again she found herself a naked captive, and once again she knew she was to be used as a sex toy by her new master. It seemed that, wherever she went, she was destined to be used as nothing more than a plaything, a source of enjoyment for men. And her own lascivious nature didn't help her aver this destiny.

The girls took her to a narrow staircase. It led up to a closed door, which Shuba opened. It clearly separated the house between the part used by the servants, and the rooms in which the owner lived. As they passed through it Lia was aware of the carpeting on the floor and the more subtle lighting. She was also aware of the uniformed servants who watched as she passed, their eyes taking in her beautiful young body.

They came to the entrance lobby, with a wide, sweeping staircase. Lia was led to the staircase and taken up. The maids took their charge along a wide landing and halted outside a door. Shuba knocked, and Lia was surprised when she heard a female voice respond.

"Come on in."

The maids opened the door, and Lia found herself in a bedroom, the walls decorated with brightly-coloured wallpaper, the bed nicely made up, with pink sheets and blankets.

But it was the occupant of the room that held her attention. There, sitting on the bed, was a stunningly beautiful Hamite woman, tall and slender, with long legs. She rose to her feet, hugged by a short silver dress that accentuated her lovely breasts. She had a classically lovely face, with high cheekbones, her eyes bright.

"Madam, this is the slave," said Shuba.

The woman moved across to where Lia was standing. Instinctively the girl took up her submissive stance, her legs spread, her hands behind her head.

"I see she has been properly trained." The woman's voice was melodic, her English perfect. "Why has she no clothes?"

"She arrived here naked," said Laska.

"She goes around like that," put in Shuba. "I think she enjoys it."

The woman smiled. "I'm sure that you are enjoying it, Shuba."

The maid looked suddenly embarrassed. "I just bathed her, Madam."

The woman walked around Lia, eyeing her closely.

"Daddy tells me he watched you being fucked by a Nilote slave," she said. "Is that true?"

Lia closed her eyes. "Yes, Madam."

"And you had an orgasm?"

"Yes Madam."

"You were fucked by a complete stranger in a public place, yet still you came?"

"Yes Madam."

The woman gave a short laugh. "You know how my father intends to use you?"

"No Madam."

"He has a farm property in the east of the country. About twenty staff and a hundred slaves work there. There are no women, so you would be an incentive. Do you understand?"

"I-I'm not sure, Madam."

"The staff will use you. They will make you work. They will thrash you if they feel you need it. And, of course, they will fuck you."

Lia felt her heart sink. It was bad enough that she was to be a sex slave. But to be used by so many?

"And of course they'll let the slaves fuck you occasionally. But I believe you would enjoy that."

Lia said nothing.

"But there is an alternative."

"Madam?"

"Maybe I could use you."

"You, Madam?"

"Yes. You could become my junior maid. Shuba and Laska would be your bosses. You would serve me like they do."

Lia looked at the woman. She could scarcely believe what she was hearing. Would this woman really make her a servant? It wasn't exactly a life she would crave, but the alternative, a slave to a gang of sex hungry men, was not something any girl could consider.

"What do you think, Shuba?" The woman turned to her maid. "Could you make use of this dirty little slut?"

The maid laughed. "Madam, you know me too well."

"What about you, Laska? Would you like to have this girl working for you?"

"Madam, if it is your wish."

There was a knock on the door.

"The woman called out something, and a reply came. Lia shivered as she recognized the voice of her new master.

"Come in, father."

The door opened and the portly man entered the room. "You are checking on my new possession?" he asked.

"Yes, father. She is wearing no clothes."

"That's how she was when I acquired her. She seems to like being naked. She walked the streets like that."

The woman laughed. "What a dirty girl."

"So what do you want? Would you like me to give her to you?"

Lia glanced at the woman, who was eyeing her up and down.

"No, father. I think she's better as a fuck machine."

The two maids burst into giggles as Lia felt her heart sink.

"So you don't want her?"

The woman shook he head. "I already have two good maids."

Lia felt tears well up in her eyes. "Please let me be your maid, Madam," she begged.

The woman shook her head. "I prefer my maids to be more modest. She's yours, father."

"Then I'll have her transported to the encampment."

A mischievous look came into his daughter's eyes. "No father, make her walk to the encampment. It will only take a few days."

The man laughed. "Walk all that way?"

"Sure. The men can ride horses. They'll be happy to do it as long as they can use her on the way."

He shook his head. "All right, honey. If that's what you want."

"And don't allow her any clothes. She should stay naked always."

"Even after she gets there?"

"Yes. She'll enjoy not wearing anything. And it'll make her easier to fuck."

The man laughed again. "Okay," he said.

Lia stared at him in horror.

"Right," said her new master to the maids, "take her and lock her up for the night. Then tell the men to get ready. They've got a long ride ahead of them."

The maids took Lia's arms and led her to the door. As they reached it, the man spoke again.

"Oh, and tell my guards they did a good job today. If any of them want the key to her cell, tell them they can tonight fuck her all they want."

# Chapter 35

Lia trudged out of the village where she had been forced to let the slave workers fuck her, and where she had subsequently been fed the spunk-garnished food. Once again the coarse rope that fastened her hands behind her and that ran between her legs was biting into her sex as the man on the horse pulled her along. As she walked she tried to ignore the laughing men and women who watched her pass, pointing at her breasts and sex, and at the spunk that dribbled from her.

As she walked she contemplated her fate. Once, just a few months ago, she had been an ordinary young lady, holding down a job, bored and hard up, but at least decent. That was before she had fallen into the hands of the Bikers. It was the Bikers who had discovered the traits in her character that even she had been unaware of. Her masochism, her exhibitionism and above all her almost limitless desire for sex.

Until she had become a Biker girl she had no idea that her body housed such enigmatic desires. It was only after the Bikers had demeaned and humiliated her that she discovered her sexual perversity. Even now, as she marched naked through this awful country her feelings were dominated by a sense of sexual arousal as she considered the sight she made.

She looked up at the man who held her leash. He was a muscular Hamite who sat proud in his saddle, occasionally glancing back at her, his expression one of contempt.

This was the kind of man to whom she now belonged. A man who saw her as a naked plaything. A cunt for his cock.

At that moment the pressure of the rope against her clitoris sent a sudden, shuddering orgasm through the naked girl. As she cried out with passion she knew her life would never be the same.

She wasn't a Biker's Girl any longer.

# The Biker's Girl Trilogy

## Biker's Girl

*Lia couldn't believe it. He wanted to spank her like some naughty schoolgirl! She hadn't been spanked since she was a child, and even then never naked. She stared at him.*

*"Over my knee," he repeated.*

*Lia struggled to think of something to say, something to prevent the humiliation he proposed to inflict upon her, but it seemed she had no choice. Slowly, reluctantly she bent over him as he sat, so that her feet and hands touched the floor on either side of the chair, her bare buttocks stretched taut over his lap...*

Set in the near future, this is the story of a beautiful young runaway who glories in sex and exhibitionism, and is an out-and-out sexual masochist.

Due to an unfortunate incident Lia is naked when she encounters a group of Bikers, and naked she remains through many painful yet erotic adventures in which she revels unashamedly.

But when the Biker of her dreams sweeps her off her feet she is surely to live happily ever after as his submissive sex slave... isn't she?

## Biker's Girl 2 - On the Run

*Once the door had closed the guard turned to look at her captive. "Such a pretty little thing," she murmured. She lifted the spear so the metal brushed Lia's cheek.*

*Lia stayed perfectly still; the point was razor sharp. The guard moved the weapon, sliding the edge down Lia's throat, making the hapless girl tremble. She slid it down her front and over her swelling breasts, just scratching her nipples, the sensation making them harden. The guard smiled and continued to tease them, the edge of the steel sending a tremor through Lia's body.*

In this second **Biker's Girl** book Lia, our beautifully submissive damsel in danger, again remains totally naked throughout, stumbling from one sexual mishap to another, pursued and hunted by numerous devious dominants and being regularly punished in all sorts of erotic ways.

And both these titles are also available as paperbacks on **AMAZON**.

www.ingramcontent.com/pod-product-compliance
Lightning Source LLC
Chambersburg PA
CBHW070751120626

46557CB00002B/539